# at Odds with the Gods

### A MYTHMATCHED / PURGATORY PLAYHOUSE CROSS-OVER

# E.J. RUSSELL

Cover art: L.C. Chase, http://lcchase.com
Edited by Meg DesCamp

ISBN: 978-1-947033-93-1

First edition
November 2023

Contact information:
ejr@ejrussell.com

# at Odds with the Gods

A MYTHMATCHED / PURGATORY
PLAYHOUSE CROSS-OVER

# E.J. RUSSELL

*Dedicated to my readers who thought Finn and Gany both deserved a chance (even if it wasn't with each other!)*

# Chapter One

Finn Lassiter's skin itched.

He wasn't sure what to blame for that. Maybe it was the antiseptic soap in the Y's shower. He'd always been sensitive to harsh cleansers, something that had been easier to manage when he'd had access to his high-end skincare products.

Maybe it was the aftermath of his bout with Hrodgar's Syndrome and his subsequent stay in the hospital. The nurses had blathered on about residual effects when he'd checked himself out against medimagical advice, but he hadn't really been listening, overwhelmed by the bone-deep need to get *away*.

Maybe it was spending every night in his wolf form, huddled under an embankment next to a creek in Forest Park. Gods, the *mud*. The *insects*. The fucking *nature*. He didn't know how his cousin Tanner had managed it for four whole months.

*You know it's not any of those things, asshole.* At least not primarily.

It was shame, plain and simple.

Shame that he'd been so oblivious and entitled for so many years that he'd *had* a high-end skincare regime. Shame that the supernatural community had nearly been wiped out because of his father's greed and arrogance. Shame that Tanner had felt he *needed* to spend all that time shifted. Because he'd been afraid.

Afraid of Finn.

Finn didn't hold that fear against Tanner, even though it wasn't justified in that particular instance. He'd wanted to *warn* him, that was all. But since Finn had pretty much been a dick to his cousin for their entire lives, he couldn't blame Tanner for not realizing his intentions for coming after him that time had been pure.

Ish.

Could Finn swear that his motives in seeking Tanner in Portland had been expressly for Tanner's benefit? Not... really? If he were honest with himself, the desire to thwart his father was a big motivator too.

Yeah. Daddy issues. *What can I say? They suck.*

As he trudged through Multnomah Village's Gabriel Park, the sole of one worn trainer gaping with every step, his phone pinged anemically, probably at the end of its charge—not a lot of power outlets in the woods, and his phone's battery was nearly as worn out as Finn was himself.

His hand shook as he pulled the phone out of his jeans, nearly losing his grip when its edge caught on the frayed hole in his pocket. He peered at the cracked screen. Two emails. He deleted the one from St. Stupid's—the hospital had been pinging him daily to get him to return for a follow-up, but that was *never* happening.

Because *they knew.*

They knew that the only reason anybody had been afflicted with Hrodgar's Syndrome at all was because Finn's father was an entitled, narcissistic asshole with empire-building ambitions and delusions of his own grandeur.

And based on Finn's behavior before he'd left his home pack for his Howling in Idaho, everybody thought he was Patrick Lassiter's spiritual heir, his son in words, beliefs, and actions rather than the result of an accidental intersection of sperm and egg. No way could he face the staff there, nurses and doctors who'd been run ragged by his father's hubris in contracting with the necromancer Hrodgar for a fucking *curse* that would force all Oregon werewolves—in fact, all weres in the Pacific Northwest—to declare fealty to the Wallowa pack alpha.

Of course, Patrick had intended to be the Wallowa pack alpha himself by that time, after murdering Tanner, the true heir. But that hadn't gone according to plan, and Hrodgar was such a shit necromancer that his curse had misfired spectacularly too, spawning a plague that affected all supes everywhere, not just Oregon werewolves, causing their very natures to turn against them.

*Hrodgar's Syndrome.* Finn supposed he was lucky they hadn't called it *Lassiter's Syndrome*, since it wouldn't have happened if Patrick hadn't wanted to be some kind of supernatural overlord.

But the real irony? That part of the curse actually worked. Yep, the authority for all werewolf packs in Oregon—hell, all supes in all of North America, and maybe the entire world and every other freaking realm, for all Finn knew—was the Wallowa pack alpha.

His cousin Tanner.

Whether he liked it or not—and from what Finn had heard, he *didn't*—Tanner Araya was the supreme alpha. If he accepted you as part of his pack, you could beat Hrodgar's Syndrome, whether the medimagical team has gotten around to treating you or not.

If Finn weren't so curdled with shame, he'd laugh himself sick.

The other message was from the werewolf council. The skin across Finn's lower back twitched and burned under the brush of his waistband, and he licked his dry lips. He'd been waiting for this message for three weeks, ever since he'd left the hospital and gone nearly feral.

His steps slowed and he huddled against the trunk of a huge oak, his finger hovering over the mail app. He inhaled until his lungs felt ready to explode, and then blew the air out in a half-whistle. *No sense delaying the inevitable.*

When he opened the email, it was... short.

*Dear Mr. Lassiter,*

*After completing our audit of the former Wallowa pack, we have found no assets explicitly belonging to you. All assets belonging to your father have been seized in restitution, and all pack assets have been remanded to Alpha Araya for distribution to former pack members. We suggest you contact Alpha Araya to arrange for your share.*

*Sincerely,*

*Lupe Moreno, secretary*

Well, that was it then. He was well and truly screwed. Broke and homeless, with no safety net. Because no way was he calling Tanner and asking him for money. He doubted Tanner would refuse him if he conjured up the balls to do it. Tanner wasn't that kind of guy, and being the alpha—the *supreme* alpha—had never been his ambition. But after the way Finn had treated him all their lives, Tanner didn't owe him squat, and no way was Finn putting Tanner in that kind of awkward position.

He'd done enough harm to his cousin already.

Finn tucked his phone away with probably more force than necessary, because he heard his pocket rip. *Great.* He only had one other change of clothes in his battered backpack, and it was in dire need of a wash, for which he didn't have the money.

*What now?* While he'd made a couple of friends during his Howling, they all belonged to Idaho packs, and *they* knew about his father now too. And since Finn had boasted about his dad's style and sophistication despite being the acting alpha of a pack whose financial roots were in the struggling timber industry, he couldn't face them now that they knew the truth. Plus, they'd probably been victims of Hrodgar's Syndrome too, so they weren't likely to be rolling in sympathy.

He wrapped his arms across his belly, pressing hard, harder, hardest. Humans had systems, didn't they? Ways for people to get help when they'd hit rock bottom? Although based on what he'd gleaned from some of the street kids he'd encountered, those systems often failed.

And anyway, he wasn't human, so he didn't really qualify.

What *did* he qualify for? It's not like he'd amassed a ton of skills while he'd been swanning around the pack house growing up, trying—and failing—to earn his father's approval by being *just like him.*

Without conscious thought, his feet had followed the same path he'd traveled since he'd gotten out of the hospital the *first* time, after he'd been treated for gunshot wounds when his father had shot him.

Twice.

Because once wasn't enough for dear old dad. Oh, no. Not when Finn threatened Patrick's power grab.

Genetics dictated so much in werewolf society, just as it did with any supe, captive to the limitations of their natures as they were, but Finn was determined *not* to be like his father. Maybe the first step was to suck it up and talk to Tanner. He wouldn't accept money. He couldn't. But after he apologized, maybe Tanner could point him in the direction of a job.

He didn't really have a choice, did he? It was Tanner or somebody else in the supe community, and strangers had less reason to think well of him than people he actually knew.

The cheerful pink-and-white-striped awning of Nectar & Ambrosia came into view beyond the trees at the edge of the park, and the iron band around Finn's chest eased.

He'd saved his meager cash everywhere else as he'd waited for the council's decision, scrimping on everything from food to clothing to housing, just so he could have *this*.

One cup of tea a day in a bright little shop scented with vanilla and cinnamon. One hour a day disconnected from his worries. One chance a day to bask in the blinding smile of the most gorgeous man Finn had ever seen.

One hour a day to be happy.

He paused outside the bakery, peering in through the gold lettering on the wide, sparkling clean window at the little round tables with their pink-and-white striped tops, the Fifties-era white heart-backed chairs, the brightly lit pastry case with its rows and rows of perfectly displayed treats—none of which Finn had ever been able to afford.

But he could smell them, and with his heightened werewolf senses, that was almost as good as tasting them.

The shop opened at six, but Finn had learned early on that Gary—the gorgeous owner and star of all Finn's erotic dreams since the moment they'd met four months ago—was always busy in the kitchen until at least eight. Then, almost like clockwork, he'd emerge from behind the swinging door with a tray of the day's special scones and give Melina, the barista, a break. Then he'd handle the register and beverage prep duties until Peyton, the other barista, arrived.

And *then* came the best part of Finn's day, the times he lived for, when Gary would take a few minutes to circulate among the tables, chatting with customers, smiling that brilliant smile, and warming the place—and Finn's heart—like a personal sun.

After the first few days, Gary always ended his rounds at Finn's table, taking the chair across from him to chat for an hour. Finn had felt guilty for monopolizing Gary's time at first, but Gary waved it off, claiming that it was his turn for a break and anyway he was the owner so he could take a little time away from the ovens if he wanted.

So Finn made sure he was at his table at precisely 8:15 every morning, and they'd been low-key flirting ever since. At least *Finn* had been flirting, although his game was definitely rusty. He'd never been certain Gary was flirting back, though, since he was just as cheerful and engaged when he talked to other customers. But they shared stories, jokes, likes and dislikes, and never seemed to run out of conversation.

From Finn's perspective, at the moment, Gary was his only friend.

Finn's fingers curled and he had to force himself to relax his fists. What if Tanner refused to give Finn a job recommendation? Or worse, what if he did, but it was away from Portland, away from easy access to Nectar & Ambrosia? Finn didn't exactly have the gold to book a Fae Transportation Association trip every day, and the FTA drivers—since the fae had been affected by Hrodgar's Syndrome too—always scowled at him like he'd turned their grandmothers to stone.

So today might be his last chance to stand at this window. His last chance to watch Gary step through the door in his pink-and-white striped apron with a tray and a smile. His last chance to confess how he felt.

His belly snarled tighter than one of Nectar & Ambrosia's cinnamon twists. What would he do if this *was* the last time? This was the only sun left in his life now. How could he survive without his daily dose of vitamin G?

Finn huffed out a breath. "Stop being such a drama llama," he muttered. "Time to get over yourself and face your shit."

But first… One last time.

# Chapter Two

"What the actual hades?" Ganymede muttered.

All the choux pastries for his eclairs were raw on the top and scorched on the bottom. He dropped the pan on the cooling rack in disgust. This was the third bake that had failed this morning, and they hadn't all failed the same way and they weren't all the same kind of pastry anyway.

His baguettes had come out looking like *briq*uettes, even though he'd baked them exactly as long and at exactly the same oven temperature as always. One pan of mini chocolate mousse cakes had fallen so hard that they looked like hockey pucks, while the other—same batter, same oven rack, same baking time—was perfectly fine.

He turned slowly, squinting at the corners of his big, airy, *perfect* kitchen, searching for signs of *them*.

The freaking Olympians.

The judgment the Fates had imposed on all twelve of them for past crimes included leaving their former victims *strictly* alone. But the gods had a history of weaseling out of the consequences of their actions. Gany should know— he'd heard them boasting about it for eons as the cupbearer on Mount Olympus, and to say he was over it was an understatement.

Technically, since Zeus was the one who'd abducted him in the first place, and who had imposed... attentions, he was Zeus's victim, so in theory, any of the others could be screwing with him now.

He sighed, pulled off his oven mitts, and hung them on their hooks. "It's not all about you, Ganymede," he muttered.

There was no reason for any of the other gods to bother with him now, and Zeus was prevented by that magical Fates-decreed restraining order from approaching Gany on the street or from stepping across the threshold of any building he occupied. So he had to face the unfortunate truth: This was a problem with the equipment. Irksome, but not sinister.

He reached into his apron pocket and pulled out his cell phone—gods, but he loved modern technology—to log a maintenance request for the oven. Before he could tuck the phone away and start a new batch of choux, an email notification popped up.

Gany's breath caught. It was from a prospective client for his catering business, which he was *still* trying to get off the ground. Granted, he hadn't put much effort into it before now, since he'd been trying to get the bakery up and operating steadily first. But now that he had Melina—who was a former Vestal, and a victim of the gods in their Roman aspect—and Portland native Peyton, who was human but so efficient they might as well be magical, Gany could finally spare some attention to expanding his footprint.

The Patterson job had been his first big proposal, and he'd *killed* the presentation if he did say so himself. He'd lowballed the bid a little—after all, he didn't strictly *need* the money. The restitution and damages the Fates had imposed on Zeus for millennia of keeping Gany captive and subjected to repeated sexual harassment was enough to make up any shortfalls for decades, even after he'd spared no expense in tricking out Nectar & Ambrosia.

But he *wanted* to cook for people. He *wanted* to see the bliss on their faces when they bit into a luscious fruit tartlet or savored a flaky za'atar croissant. And this could be it. The springboard. The launching pad. The spark that ignited his future.

Fingers trembling, he opened the message.

*Dear Mr. Mead,*
*Thank you for your presentation. Your Mediterranean offerings were delicious, but we have decided to go in another direction.*
*Sincerely,*
*Martha Patterson*

Gany stared at the screen for a full thirty seconds, sure that it couldn't be right. Another direction? They'd specifically *demanded* a Mediterranean-inspired menu, and Gany had *nailed* it. They said so. Right *there*. Granted, Mediterranean was his comfort zone, considering that's where he'd come from—*three thousand years ago*. But he'd *diversified* since then. He could serve up any number of other cuisines, but only if they weren't bundled away in some hidden client agenda.

"What is this *other direction* of which you speak?" Gany muttered. Maybe if they told him, he could present an alternative menu and they'd—

"Knock knock?"

At the cheerful greeting from the kitchen door, Gany nearly fumbled his phone. He pasted on a smile, though, and it wasn't even difficult, because he was *always* happy to see TD Baylor, the man who was responsible for calling the gods on their shit and springing Gany from eternal cupbearer duty.

"TD. Hey." Gany tucked his phone away. He probably shouldn't respond to the client when his hair was on virtual fire anyway.

TD walked into the kitchen. "Sorry to barge in, but Melina said you were back here."

"No worries." Gany held his arms wide. "As long as I get a hug for my trouble."

TD chuckled and beckoned Gany forward, something Gany was always grateful for: TD always waited for Gany to instigate contact first. So Gany snuggled close and wrapped his arms around TD's waist, heaving a sigh when TD returned the embrace. TD gave the best hugs. His boyfriend was *so* lucky.

"I've got the keys for you, house and car both."

Gany reluctantly stepped back. "I don't need the car keys. I don't drive. Not yet."

TD shrugged. "All the same, we didn't want to leave you without them in case of emergencies. If you need to take Sir, Bear, or Ozzie to the vet or anything, maybe Peyton or Melina could drive you."

Gany peered up into TD's narrow, clever face. "Is something wrong with the boys? Are they sick?"

"Not really, but they're a little anxious at the moment. They caught Lonnie packing our suitcases and drew appropriate conclusions about imminent separation." He shook his head, chuckling. "They've tried to guilt us into staying with those big puppy dog eyes, but this role is too good for Lonnie to pass up, especially since I'm on the FX crew so we can be together on set for the whole shoot. I'll warn you, though, the pups have reached that rambunctious teenage phase. Their feet are too big for them to manage, and they have a tendency to run into things, including each other. We've moved everything breakable to higher ground, just in case."

Gany gave him a look of mock outrage. "How dare you impugn my godpuppies that way? They are *angels*."

"Angels?" TD's mouth curled in a familiar sardonic half smile. "They used to guard the gates of hell, Gany."

Gany sniffed. "That was *before*, and they didn't have a lot of choice, did they?"

"True enough." He rubbed the back of his neck. "But they're working dogs, Gany. They're used to having a purpose. I don't think they'll be happy being ordinary earthside dogs once they're fully grown, and I'm a little worried how Lonnie and I will manage."

"You'll figure it out."

"I hope so." He peered down at Gany, his eyebrows bunched in obvious concern. "You sure you're up for this gig? Location filming is scheduled to go on for at least four months. If it's a problem, I can pull out—"

"No! You and Lonnie should be together. I can handle the boys. Gimme those keys."

"If you're sure?" At Gany's emphatic nod, TD passed him the key ring. "You've got both our numbers, and if you can't reach us immediately, you can contact the agency. Echo can get a message to us through the production company."

Gany shook his head. "I still can't believe Echo started her own talent agency."

TD chuckled. "She's amazing." He winked. "Of course, it didn't hurt that her first client was as high-end as Lonnie Coleridge, and that she landed him the lead in a hit series and its movie spinoffs right out of the gate. She's got a waitlist as long as—"

"Your dick?" Gany said, fluttering his eyelashes.

TD cocked one eyebrow. "I was going to say Prometheus's arm, thank you."

Heat rushed up Gany's throat, and he ducked his head, biting his lip. "I'm sorry. I should know better than anybody not to make inappropriate sexual comments."

TD's expression softened. "Since I doubt Zeus restricted his inappropriate sexual behavior to *comments*, I'll never call you out on a little frisky language, Gany."

The heat on Gany's cheeks somehow migrated to fill his chest with warmth. *Friends. They were the best.*

"Thanks, hon. I appreciate that more than you know." He donned a saucy smirk and winked. "Besides, it's a lot more fun to tease you when Lonnie's around to look all protective and possessive."

TD grinned. "Amen to that." He opened his arms and Gany stepped in for another hug. "Thanks again for doing this. And if you want anyone to stay with you, if it would make you feel better or safer, there's plenty of room."

Gany peered up at him. "Safer? Is there something you know that I don't?"

"I don't trust the gods," TD growled. "Especially that asshole Zeus."

"Don't worry." He patted TD's chest. "He can't come near me without violating the terms of his parole, and then *he'd* be the one staked out on a rock getting his liver snacked on every day. I'm fine."

"Still. The offer stands. Treat the house as your home while we're gone. Okay?"

"Okay." He made a shooing motion. "Now go, before you miss your plane. Give Lonnie a kiss from me."

"Will do." TD lifted a hand in farewell and headed for the back door. "Whoa!"

He dodged to the side as the door swung open with a clang and Peyton barreled inside.

"Oh, sorry, TD!" they panted. "You okay?"

"Fine, Peyton." He waved at Gany again. "See you in a few months, Gany." He glanced at Peyton. "I mean, *Gary*."

"It's all right, TD," Gany said. "Melina and Peyton know my other name. Have a good trip. I expect many, *many* spoiler reels from you during filming."

"You got it." He left, closing the door carefully with a snick of its metal panic bar.

Gany faced Peyton, both eyebrows lifted. "A gracious good morning to you. A little early, aren't you?"

Peyton gulped down air. "I had to— You need to— There's a—"

"Slow down, slow down." Gany took Peyton by the elbow and led them to a tall stool next to the stand mixer. "Catch your breath, okay?" He peered at Peyton's shirt. "And not to be a persnickety boss, but you should probably change your shirt before your shift. You're covered in cat hair."

"I don't have a cat, although I do have a sugar glider."

"I didn't know you had a pet. Can we meet them sometime?"

"Not a pet," Peyton wheezed.

"Not a pet?" Gany frowned. "But—"

"Never mind that." Peyton patted their backpack. "I've got spare clothes in here, but I didn't have time to change before I jetted out of my apartment."

"Okay." Gany grabbed the pitcher of filtered water from the staff fridge and poured Peyton a glass. "Drink a little of this and tell me what's got your pants on fire this morning."

Peyton gulped down half the water and then took a huge breath, their narrow shoulders lifting. "You want to get into wedding cakes, right?"

Gany's eyebrows drew together. "Yeeesss," he said, drawing out the word. "That's the plan. To tie the bakery to the catering business." *Once I've got a catering business.*

"Well, I've got a lead on an opportunity for a cake."

Gany wrestled with a bump of excitement, because... "A *lead* on an *opportunity*? That sounds... nebulous. A couple of steps removed from an actual booking."

"No, the booking is real. I mean, if you want the gig, you've got it." Peyton fumbled a folded paper out of their jeans pocket. "The details are here. Size, flavors, yada yada."

Gany took the paper and unfolded it. As he read, his eyebrows rose farther up his forehead. So much for nebulous. "This is actually... really specific." And specific was good. But in addition, it gave him leeway for his own special touches. "And this is definite? They want the cake for certain?"

Peyton nodded. "Absolutely." They grimaced. "There's a catch, though."

Gany sighed. Of course there was a catch. "What? I have to pass a tasting test with the entire bridal party and their extended families?"

"No. It's just..." Peyton crooked both elbows at their sides, palms flat in a *what can I say* shrug. "It's a backup cake."

"A backup cake?"

"Yeah. In case the first one, I don't know, *fails* somehow."

"So what you're saying is... it's possible *nobody* will taste it? Like at all?"

Peyton nodded again. "Yeah."

Gany chewed on his lower lip. While he loved the process of cooking and baking, he didn't consider it a solo performance. The diners' enjoyment was half the reason for him to prepare anything. Maybe eons of serving the same damn thing to a pantheon of gods who understood gratitude even less than they did consent had left its mark.

He brandished the paper. "How did you find out about this anyway?"

"Friend of a friend. Of a friend. Of a— Does it really matter?"

"I suppose not." It was a fantastic break, but it would be such a *waste*.

"They'll pay for it, even if they don't use it. So, I mean, there's that."

Peyton had a point. Besides, even if nobody ate the cake —and somehow, Gany would make sure that people had that opportunity, even if it was just the serving staff— Gany would have established a foothold in the wedding cake space as somebody who could deliver.

"Okay. I'll do it. Is there somebody I need to—"

"I'll let them know you're in. Del—they're one of the nearlyweds—will probably give you a call. You can discuss it with them, ask them any questions. Although..." There was that shrug again. "They did ask that you keep this confidential. Like from everybody else in the wedding party."

Gany frowned. "Even from their partner?" Peyton nodded. "That seems a little sketchy."

"It looks that way, but I know Del. They're a good person. If they want it kept secret, they've got a really good reason." Peyton blinked wide, brown eyes at Gany. "Please?"

Gany chuckled. "Oh stop. I'll have enough puppy dog eyes to endure with Sir, Bear, and Ozzie. You know, from *actual puppies.*" *Even though they used to be a single three-headed dog.* "I don't need them from my employees too."

"So you'll do it?"

"Of course I will."

"Yay!" Peyton clapped their hands and jumped off the stool. "I'll just tell—"

"Hssst!" Melina poked her head around the door. "He's heeere!"

And Gany's heart jolted all the way to his throat. "F-Finn?"

"Who else?"

Peyton nudged Gany's ribs with an extremely sharp elbow. "You asked him out yet?"

Gany planted his fists on his hips. "Will you two stop trying to set me up? I don't have *time* to date." Not to mention the inclination, since the residual trauma from literally millennia of sexual harassment wasn't the best foundation for a relationship. His therapist was helping him work through his issues, though, and when he looked into Finn's sad, soft eyes, he thought he might *almost* be ready.

Maybe.

Dr. Kendrick had told him that he wasn't required to conform to anybody's timeline but his own, that he could pick the ways he felt comfortable to ease into intimacy. A little daily flirting with the counter or a table between them was... safe, and gradually, over the last few months, the feeling in Gany's midsection when he thought of Finn touching him—or of him touching *Finn*—had morphed from writhing adders to joyous butterflies.

He glanced down at his apron. *Ewww.* The cheerful pink and white stripes were splotched with brown and red, and though it was only chocolate, vanilla, and raspberry sauce, the colors conjured up more ominous scenarios.

Gany untied it and yanked it over his head to toss into the laundry bag. "How do I look? Is my hair okay?" He rubbed his nose. "Do I have flour all over my face."

Melina slanted a smile and patted his hair. "You look adorable, as usual."

"Thanks." Gany blew out a breath between pursed lips. "Here I go."

As he turned, he heard Peyton mutter, "No time to date, my ass," followed by Melina's snicker.

He ignored them and pushed through the swinging door into the storefront.

# Chapter Three

As soon as the door closed behind him, welcoming him into the bakery with a tinkle of its little brass bell, tension seeped out of Finn's shoulders. He closed his eyes and took a deep breath, and there it was: vanilla, cinnamon, coffee, citrus, and... His nose twitched. Underlying the delicious aromas he expected was the smell of scorched pastry and burnt chocolate, things he'd never detected at Nectar & Ambrosia before.

He shrugged it off. Every baker, even someone as talented as Gary, probably had off days. After all, nobody was perfect.

He inhaled again, his were senses seeking that seductive scent that was Gary and Gary alone: honey-sweet, with the tang of mint and salt, like a beehive in a garden overlooking the sea.

Melina was still behind the counter, steaming milk for a... cappuccino, according to Finn's nose. She grinned at him before turning to say something to the customer.

Finn glanced around. As usual at this time of day, the shop's tables were mostly empty, since humans were on their way to work. Later on in the morning, people would drift in with friends or books or laptops, to settle in for a longer stay.

Finn edged toward his usual table, a two-top tucked into the far corner next to the end of the pastry case. He was early—it wasn't even eight yet, so Gary wouldn't be out for a chat for at least twenty minutes.

*Shit.* If he'd taken longer walking through the park, he'd still have an excuse: *Can't call Tanner now, not when Gary could appear at any moment, because that would be rude.*

But that tactic wouldn't work this morning. His eagerness for the bakery's sensory hug, his desperation for Gary's smile, had cut his stellar avoidance skills off at the knees.

*Stop putting it off, asshole. You don't have a choice anymore.*

He sat on the edge of the chair facing the back wall, shoulders hunched, phone cradled in both palms, and pulled up Tanner's contact. He took a steadying breath, fingers hovering over the screen.

*For fuck's sake, just do it.*

He jabbed the screen and then held the phone gingerly to his ear.

It rang once, twice, three times. Four. Finn was about to hang up when it connected.

"Hi, this is Tanner Araya."

"Hey, Tanner, it's—"

"I'm sorry I can't take your call right now—" *Fuck. Voicemail.* "—as I'm away for a week at a conference. If you need assistance before I return, please call the Portland Howling Residence at this number"—he rattled off the digits and Finn scrabbled a pencil stub out of his pocket to jot them on a napkin—"and someone will help you right away. If you can wait, please leave a message and I'll get back to you at my first opportunity. Thank you."

Finn disconnected before the beep, because fuck if he was going to beg over voicemail. But now what?

While he could probably last another week spending his nights as a wolf and showering at the Y, he really couldn't face *hunting* as a wolf, and after today's tea, he wouldn't have money for anything else.

Maybe he should bypass the tea this morning. Not that three bucks would get him very far anywhere else, but at least his wallet wouldn't be totally empty.

He glanced down at the napkin. The pencil had torn it in two places when he'd scribbled the number, but it was still legible. *There goes another excuse.*

The Portland Howling Residence—aka, the Doghouse. Would someone there be able to help him? The other guys from Tanner's Howling knew a little too much about Finn's dad, not to mention Finn himself. Tanner didn't live at the Doghouse anymore, though, so maybe the guys who knew him would have graduated too. Besides what other option did he have?

So he dialed the number. The call connected right away, but instead of a greeting, there was a clatter and a muffled *woof*. Then the sound of unmistakable fumbling, followed by a very young-sounding voice.

"Hello, this is the Doghouse and I'm Noah—"

"Noah," said another, older voice, "what have we said about answering the phone?"

"But it was *ringing*, Jordan, and you were in the *bathroom.*"

"It rang one time, and I was already— Oh, crap." More fumbling. "Hello?"

"Sorry," Finn mumbled. "Wrong number."

He hung up. *Jordan*. He was one of Tanner's friends. He'd *been there* that day at Wildwood, when Finn's father had shot him and tried to kill Tanner. That was a little too close to the bone for Finn to handle. But again, what other option did he have? He had no room for stupid pride anymore.

He sighed, letting his forehead drop against the cracked screen in his hand. Maybe if he—

"Here you go. Your usual."

Finn startled, breath catching, rearing back in his chair as an enameled tray complete with teapot and cup *thlick*ed onto the table in front of him.

"Oh, I'm sorry." Gary gazed down at him from those dark, dark eyes, his teeth denting his full lower lip and his black curls tumbled across his forehead. "I didn't mean to scare you."

*Oh shit*. Now he didn't have a choice but to pay, and *double shit*—there was a cinnamon twist on the little tray too. He definitely didn't have the cash to pay for *that*.

Despite alarm rolling around his middle like a tumbleweed, though, his heart warmed. *Gary knows my usual*. Unless it was Melina, since she was the one who usually took his order. But he'd never ordered a pastry so—

"Are you okay?" Gary sank down in the chair opposite him. "If you don't mind my saying so, you're looking a little rough."

Finn chuckled weakly and ran his hands through his too-shaggy hair. "Yeah. Sorry about that. I don't mean to bring down the ambiance around here."

Gary frowned, and even *that* was beautiful. "That's not what I mean by rough. I mean, you look a little upset."

In the face of Gary's obvious concern, the last remnants of Finn's pride crumbled. "I, um, got a disappointing email this morning. It's... not good."

"You're not the only one. Nothing like starting the morning with crummy news to really set the tone for the day, right?" Gary glanced down at the tea tray. "Shoot, I shouldn't have assumed. Maybe you were going to order something different today."

*Fuck it.* "Actually, I'm not in a position to order anything." He tapped his back pocket. "I can't pay. I'm sorry. I really shouldn't have come in at all. I should go."

He struggled to rise, his chair screeching against the tiles as he pushed it back.

"No. Please." Gary reached across the table and grasped Finn's forearm. "Don't go." He nodded at the tray. "This is on the house."

"I couldn't—"

"Not like I can serve it to anybody else. If you don't accept it, I'll have to toss it." He widened his eyes in total faux innocence. "That's the finest Assam and one of my signature pastries. You wouldn't want to *waste* them, would you?"

Finn narrowed his own eyes. "Guilt tripping much?"

Gary's smile dawned, dimples peeping in his cheeks. "Is it working?"

Finn swallowed against a square-feeling lump. *That's what swallowing your pride feels like, I guess.* "I don't really have the room to refuse. So thank you. Although..." *In for a penny.* "I'd feel much better about this if you'd join me with your own beverage of choice."

Gary nodded appreciatively. "Nice job avoiding assumptions. I'll be right back."

Finn's gaze followed him as he rose and trotted around the pastry case toward where Melina and Peyton both stood behind the counter.

*Gods, he's so beautiful.* Back in the day, when Finn's ego and heir-presumptive sense of entitlement had given him a false sense of his due, he would have made a play for Gary. But now? He had nothing to offer anybody, even himself.

So he turned back to his own tea and poured a cup, doctoring it with a packet of raw sugar and a dollop of cream.

As he took the first blessed sip, Gary slid another tray onto the table, this one with another teapot and cup and a plate of assorted scones.

"There," Gary said. "Now we're set."

Finn inhaled and closed his eyes, letting the aroma of lemon, cardamom, nutmeg, and Gary infuse his senses.

"Gods, I'm going to miss it here."

"Miss it?" The sharp note in Gary's voice made Finn open his eyes. "Why are you going to miss it?"

Finn lifted his cup and took a gulp of tea that seared his tonsils and made his eyes water. "I, um, might be leaving the area."

"Might be or are definitely?"

"I... don't know?" Finn broke off a corner of his cinnamon twist and popped it in his mouth to give him time to come up with a better answer. "Like I said, I'm broke. I'm gonna have to beg my cousin for a handout and a place to stay, and hope he's generous enough to agree."

"You think he won't be?"

Finn shrugged, chasing a pastry crumb around the plate with a fingertip. "He has no reason *to* be. I mean, he's a nice guy, but I was an asshole to him the whole time we were growing up. He'd be totally justified in telling me to take a hike."

"Is that likely?"

Finn sighed. He was still a werewolf, and pack was pack, but did that count if your pack didn't exist anymore? "I don't know."

"What about other family? Other friends?"

"That's... complicated."

"Does this have anything to do with whatever happened in June?"

Finn blinked. "June?" June was when Hrodgar's Syndrome flared up, but how did Gary—

"You didn't come in the shop for thirteen days." Gary's cheeks flushed a perfect rose. "I, um, may have noticed."

A hum started low in Finn's belly, something he didn't recognize, it had been so long since he'd felt anything like it. *Gratification.* "You did?"

"I did. So if you want to talk about any of it?" Gary propped his chin on his fist, his gaze soft. "I'm a good listener."

Again, Finn thought *fuck it.* He held on to that hum of gratification, the knowledge that Gary had noticed him, maybe even *missed* him, and took the leap.

"My father is... a criminal. He did some really bad shit and hurt a lot of people. Friends. Family. Even strangers." *Me included.* "He's in... prison now, but I doubt any of his victims would be willing to forget and forgive enough to give his son anything but a kick in the ass."

"Ugh." Gary leaned back. "Daddy issues. Trust me, I get it. I also get how people can misdirect their hurt and anger toward someone whose only guilt is proximity. Who's just as much a victim as they are themselves."

Finn blinked. "Th-thank you."

Gary's expression turned almost warlike, and somehow didn't seem out of place on his face, or make him any less beautiful. "Did your cousin refuse to help you?"

"No. Not yet." Finn gazed down at his tea. "I, um, haven't actually asked him."

"Maybe you should do that. No sense abandoning hope until you've pursued all your options. Even Pandora got that."

Finn's eyebrows bunched. *What the...* "Pandora?"

Gary's gaze flicked away and he waved on hand airily. "Never mind. The point is, don't anticipate the worst."

"Why not?" Finn said morosely. "If I expect the worst but get something that's a couple of steps above that, it'd be a win. Yay," he said, deadpan.

Gary waggled a finger at him. "You, sir, are far too fatalistic. Now, here's what we're going to do—"

"We?" Finn's fingers tightened around his teacup, the warmth under his hands matching the dawning warmth in his chest.

"Of course, we. You've been my most consistent customer ever since I opened the bakery." He flushed again. "Chatting with you every morning is one of the highlights of my day, so *we* definitely want to keep you around to brighten future days as well." His eyebrows quirked, pinching above his perfectly straight, perfectly adorable nose. "That is, if you *want* to keep brightening the days."

Their gazes met and held. Finn knew how to breathe, he was sure, because he wasn't a *vampire*. He required oxygen. But somehow he had no clue how to get air into his lungs. His vision swam, but through the dark spots, he could see Gary's expression turning from inquisitive to alarmed.

"Finn, are you— Gods damn it, I don't even know your last name, or who I should call in an emergency, but you need to—"

"Lassiter," he croaked and at last was able to suck in a breath. "My last name's Lassiter."

He tensed, waiting for the reaction, the revulsion, the withdrawal. But it didn't come. Instead, Gary patted his hand and smiled.

"Excellent. While it doesn't look like you're about to pass out anymore, it's good to know."

Of course Gary wouldn't know the infamous Lassiter name and why so many had reason to revile it. *Because he's human.*

Which was both a blessing and a curse. A blessing because, hey, no reviling. But a curse because of the damned Secrecy Pact: No one in the supernatural community could reveal their existence to a human under pain of extreme punishment. Any hope Finn harbored for a deeper relationship with Gary would be based on a lie because he'd never be able to tell Gary the truth about his nature.

Gary grinned, planting his palms on the table. "Now that you're feeling more the thing, why don't you contact your cousin and find out what he is or is not willing to do for you, and we'll go from there."

Finn jerked his chin at his phone's cracked screen. "I actually tried to reach him, but he's away for another week."

"Hmmm." Gary tapped his full lower lip with a finger. "Then what about—"

"Ganymede!" a voice boomed from the doorway.

A tall guy—Remus's balls, he had to be at least six-eight —with smooth golden skin, wavy black hair, and flashing dark eyes strode over to Finn's table. Despite looking like a classical Greek statue, the guy was wearing blue chinos, work boots, and a green T-shirt from one of the nurseries out in Washington County.

The guy planted himself next to Gary, brandishing a cell phone. "Ganymede, you have to—"

"*Hell*-o," Gary said, scrambling out of his chair to take the guy by the elbow. "*Aaron.*"

The guy—Aaron, apparently—wrinkled his perfect brow and gazed down at Gary. "What?"

Gary chuckled breathlessly and looked down at Finn. "Who's named Ganymede anyway. Silly name."

He hauled Aaron toward the kitchen door, a feat since Aaron had at least a foot in height and the muscles straining his T-shirt were... a lot. Aaron, however, didn't fight back, just waved his phone some more.

"Ga—"

"Ah!" Gary cut him off with a sharp syllable. "In the *kitchen*. Now." He paused for a moment and looked back at Finn. "Don't go anywhere? Please?"

"Um, sure."

Gary's tense expression relaxed into his usual brilliant smile. "Excellent. I'll be right back."

# Chapter Four

Gany hauled Eros through the swinging door into the kitchen just as Peyton was removing a sheet of shortbread cookies from the oven.

"Peyton, could you help Melina out front for a bit, please?" He glanced at Eros, who was frowning at his phone. "I just need a minute." *And it had better not be any longer than that.*

Ever since Purgatory Playhouse had been shut down, Gany had been blissfully free of the sight of any Olympian. Suddenly here one was, just when he was finally getting a chance to make some time with his crush.

"Ga—"

"Do not speak." Gany held up a palm as Peyton set the cookie sheet on the cooling rack. He waited until they'd cleared the door and then dropped both fists to his hips. "What in hades are you *doing* here? Do you *want* an eagle to chow down on your liver for the next thousand years? You're not allowed to be anywhere *near* your victims."

"Victims." Eros scoffed. "I didn't have *victims*. I had *giftees*."

"Tell that to Medea. Tell that to Medea's *children*."

"None of them are here, and I didn't do anything to *you*."

Gany folded his arms, eyes narrowing. "No? I'm still not convinced you and your stupid arrows weren't behind Zeus's obsession with me."

"*Anyway*," Eros said airily and then shoved his phone under Gany's nose. "Have you *seen* this?"

"I'm not seeing it now, considering it's practically up my left nostril."

Eros grabbed for Gany's hand. Breath frozen, Gany stumbled backward, barely managing to suppress a scream, and smacked his hip on the corner of the marble pastry counter. He wrapped his arms across his stomach and tried not to hyperventilate.

Eros frowned for a second and then, surprisingly, looked apologetic and offered the phone to Gany on his palm.

Gany settled his breathing and edged forward to take it. He peered down at the gigantic device, twice as big as Gany's own phone.

*Trust an Olympian to supersize things.*

The inner snark calmed him further, enough that he was able to focus on the screen. It displayed an extremely realistic looking mountain, its peak crowned in clouds, with a light brown path zigzagging up between a maze of trees, rocks, bushes, and the occasional sheep. A male figure in a loincloth, dark curls tamed by a cloth tied across his forehead, stood near the foot of the mountain, his hands braced against a boulder taller than he was.

"What is this?"

"It's the Divine Dues app."

Gany looked up at the disgust in Eros's voice. "It's the what?"

Eros huffed a breath. "The *Divine Dues* app. It's how we're supposed to know when we've done enough to get back to Olympus."

Gany's lips slid sideways into a smirk. "I take it this graphic is supposed to represent Olympus?"

Eros nodded. "And that's my avatar. Every time I do something that the app considers a step toward paying my dues, I push the boulder further up the mountain."

Gany peered at the screen again. "Eros. You're at the absolute bottom of the mountain."

"I *know*." Eros snatched the phone back and swiped his finger on the screen, rotated it to landscape mode, then held it up. "Look at this."

The screen depicted twelve columns, each with a stylized mountain and a progress bar topped by a boulder icon. The Olympians' names were displayed above each mountain. Gany was interested to see that most of the boulder icons, including Eros's, were bottomed out.

Eros shook the phone. "That prig Hestia is three quarters of the way there. It's not fair! She started out with an advantage. How much trouble can you get in hanging around a hearth?"

"You'd be surprised," Gany said dryly.

Eros stared at the screen morosely. "How am I supposed to make any progress when I'm stuck working at a flaming *nursery*. Nothing but plants, plants, plants." He held up his other hand and waggled his fingers. "I've got *dirt* under my *fingernails*."

Gany rolled his eyes. "You could always try washing your hands and using a nail brush."

"Why should I have to?" he said sulkily. "I never did before."

"Yes, well, the days of regular nymph manicures are in the past. Get over it."

"Why can't I redeem myself by working at something I'm good at?" Eros closed the Divine Dues app with a petulant swipe. "I could work at a matchmaking agency. Or, like bartend at a singles bar." He scowled at his phone. "Although these stupid *dating* apps are encroaching on my turf. It's like people don't even *need* me anymore."

"Newsflash, Eros. We didn't need you before."

He looked up and his expression morphed from sullen to smug. "Oh really?" He waggled his eyebrows. "Valentine's Day!"

"What?"

"I'm *celebrated*. There are *songs* about me." His face scrunched up. "Although they use that ridiculous Roman name. Cupid. *Pfaugh*. But it's still me. On *greeting cards*."

"Most of those greeting card pics are of a chubby naked baby with wings."

He sniffed. "Artistic license."

"Uh huh. Now seriously. Why are you here?"

"I told you. I need to pay my dues, like *now*, and this?" He gestured to his T-shirt. "This is not gonna get me there before that bastard Hermes." His perfect jaw firmed. "I should be doing what I'm best at. Helping people fall in love."

"You didn't *help* people. You *forced* them."

"Po-tay-to, po-tah-to."

"Not po-tay-to. Not po-tah-to. No spuds of any kind. You're supposed to be *learning* from this, Eros." Gany pointed at the phone. "If the only reason you're trying to do good is because you want to beat somebody else to the finish line, then you're missing the whole point."

"I can do good and still be me." Eros brightened and jerked his head toward the swinging door. "That guy out there, the one who was moping into his tea? I could make him a project. I bet he'd cheer up if he got a little nookie."

"No," Gany barked. "Absolutely not. You leave him alone completely. No manipulating humans." *And definitely no manipulating Finn.*

Eros's smile turned sly. "But if I didn't manipulate a *human*—"

"If you manipulate his tea into his lap or a dog into his path or a... a... I don't know, *banana peel* that he slips on and falls into somebody's arms, it still counts as interference. Eros, you're *not allowed.*"

"Oh, come on, Gany. There are more dating apps than I can count. These mortals are *desperate* to find love, and who better than me to help them? But if I *engage*, I'll move the boulder and leave Hestia in the dust!"

"Eros, don't make me contact the Fates."

"Come on, Gany," he whined. "At this rate, Zeus will show up to take you home before I'm even halfway there."

"Home?" Gany blinked at him. "I *am* home."

"You mean here?" Eros glanced around the bakery, Gany's pride and joy. "But... but you live on Olympus."

"No. I *existed* on Olympus. Because I was *abducted*. But here, I'm *home*." Gany shook a finger under Eros's nose. "And if Zeus gets any bright ideas about carrying me off again, remind him that the Fates don't *care* that he was the king. He can't go back to the old ways. None of you can. Let us go, Eros. Give us our lives back and leave us alone."

"You need us." He waved his phone. "The apps don't lie."

"No, what we need is self-determination."

"We're gods," he said, his tone bewildered. "Obviously we know what's best for you."

"Seriously?" Gany threw up his hands. "Consent is a thing. It's *important*. It's *critical*, something you all need to understand."

"But—"

"Did Zeus *ask* if I wanted to get hauled up to Olympus on the wings of an eagle to spend eternity bussing the gods' table? No, he did not. Did Hades *ask* Persephone if she wanted to forsake the sun for half the year to play house with the dead? No, he did not. Did Daphne *ask* Apollo to chase her through the woods until her father had the brilliant notion of turning her into a tree? No, she did not." Gany narrowed his eyes. "As a matter of fact, that last one was your fault anyway. Another instance of the collateral damage of your petty godlet one-upmanship."

Eros scrunched up his face. "Okay, that's fair, I guess. I didn't really think that one through, but Apollo totally deserved—"

"Eros," Gany said through clenched teeth, "Apollo is not the one who suffered. And you *didn't care.*"

"Okay, okay. Fine. I can do better. You'll see."

Eros spun and whisked out the kitchen door before Gany could protest. He huffed an exasperated sigh. Thank the Fates Eros didn't have his bow with him, because...

Gany's heart bounded toward his throat. *Shit.* Eros might not have his bow, but did he still have arrows?

"No, no, no." Gany rushed through the door in time to see Eros, one hand curled as though he were holding something, stalking toward Finn, who was seated facing the back wall as usual.

Gany quickly dodged in front of him just as Finn glanced over his shoulder, eyebrows lifted in question. Gany's smile was probably a cross between anemic and desperate. "Excuse me for a minute, please, Finn?"

Finn's gaze darted to Eros for an instant. "Sure." He turned away again, an unreadable expression on his face.

Gany faced Eros again. "What are you *doing*?" he whispered.

Eros snatched his hands behind his back. "Nothing."

Gany held up his palm and curled his fingers with a *gimme* motion. "Come on. Hand it over."

Eros scowled, his perfect eyebrows bunched, and for a moment, Gany thought he'd refuse. If that happened, it wasn't as though Gany could do anything about it. Even if tackling somebody in the middle of his shop weren't a total customer service fail, Eros was built like an Ionic column. Gany's entire weight probably couldn't budge him an inch.

Luckily, Eros heaved a god-sized sigh and held out his fist. When he uncurled his fingers…

"Are you *serious* right now?" Gany hissed. "A *coffee stirrer*?" He *knew* he shouldn't have gone for the ones shaped like little spears. He snatched it off Eros's palm, grabbed his elbow, and marched him out the front door, the tinkle of the bell for once more ominous than cheerful.

Once they were outside, however, Gany's options were limited, since pedestrian traffic had picked up. He dropped Eros's elbow and pasted on a smile, nodding at a couple of his regulars as they headed into Nectar & Ambrosia. As soon as they'd stepped inside, though, he poked Eros in the chest.

"I told you. Do not mess with him. You're *not allowed.*"

"But look at him, Gany." Eros all but pressed his nose against the window. "He's pathetic. He needs a distraction, and nothing's a better distraction than love."

"Maybe, when it's our own choice and not *imposed* on us by somebody else's agenda."

Gany glanced at Finn, his shoulders slumped as he hunched over his tea, then back at Eros, whose avid gaze hadn't wavered. The gods all had the impulse control of a sleep-deprived toddler, so Gany didn't trust Eros not to make another try at Finn, lying in wait for him and forcing him into a lust-struck obsession with some stranger. Given Finn's current crappy situation, that could only end in further disaster for the poor guy.

Gany chewed on his lip. Should he? Well, why not? He didn't have Fates-ordered dues to pay, but that didn't mean he couldn't do something nice for someone. Help someone. He glanced at Eros again, who was actually pressing his nose on the glass, fogging it up under the gold ampersand. *Protect someone.*

"Listen up, Eros. You are not to enter my shop again without my permission."

Eros glance down at him. "Why'd you name the place Nectar & Ambrosia then, if you hated your life on Olympus so much?"

"It's *ironic.* Although everyone who comes here thinks it's metaphorical." He poked Eros in the ribs. "Do you understand me? You're banished from my shop."

His gaze returned to Finn. "Yeah, yeah. Whatever."

"I'm staying at TD and Lonnie's house, and you're not allowed to come in there either."

That caught his attention. "I couldn't anyway. They've got Cerberus. He won't let us in."

Gany blinked. He hadn't realized the pups were a security measure, but it made sense. The gods were vindictive assholes, and TD and Lonnie were the reasons they were having to answer for their actions. Although apparently the gods didn't know that instead of a giant three-headed dog, Cerberus was now three large, extremely rambunctious puppies.

"Well. Good." He pointed at Eros's nose. "See you remember that. Now go away."

Gany marched back into the shop, hoping—for several reasons—that Finn would say yes to his proposal.

# Chapter Five

After Gary hauled that big, buff guy outside, Finn had huddled over his tea, disappointment swamping him.

*Obviously,* somebody as beautiful as Gary would already have a boyfriend. The brief flare of hope in Finn's chest when Gary had seemed so sympathetic, so sincerely interested in his problems needed to *die.*

"Pandora should have shut the freaking box," he muttered at his cinnamon twist before taking a vicious bite. Nothing was worse than hope because it made you *want,* want things you could never have.

"You don't really mean that, do you?"

Finn jerked his head up to find Gary gazing down at him with those warm, dark eyes. "I, um, what?"

He slid into the chair across from Finn. "That the world —that you—would be better off without hope." He sighed, his gaze shifting beyond Finn's shoulder and his eyebrows pinching for a moment before he met Finn's eyes again and smiled. "Things can be dark enough. Imagine how much darker they would be if we never tried to *fix* them, and nobody will even *try* to fix them if they don't think they can succeed."

Finn nudged his teacup widdershins, until its handle pointed at precisely three o'clock. "Some things are too big to fix."

"That's what I used to think, but you know what? Miracles can happen when you least expect them. I'm total proof of that."

Gary's tone, fierce and joyful all at once, made Finn look up. "You are?"

Gary nodded solemnly. "I spent *millennia*—I mean what *seemed* like millennia trapped in a... a dead-end job with the *worst* boss. I thought I'd never escape. But then somebody flipped the script and"—he spread his palms with a flourish—"here I am. Free. Doing something I'd been dreaming of for *eons*."

"Eons?" Finn quirked a smile. "That long, eh?"

Gary rolled his eyes. "You have *no* idea. But my point is that hope snuck in when I least expected it, thanks to someone I never saw coming."

"Ah." Finn jerked his teacup another quarter turn, rattling its saucer. "That guy who was just here? Aaron, was it?"

Gary blinked. "What? Oh, gods, no."

"So... He's not your boyfriend?"

"*Definitely* not." He frowned. "He didn't approach you, did he?"

With a shrug, Finn tapped the cup's handle. *Seven o'clock. Eight o'clock. Eight-thirty.* "No reason why he should."

Gary drummed his fingers on the table, eyes narrowed. Then he seemed to reach some kind of decision, because his expression cleared and he squared his shoulders. "This may seem weird, but how would you like to stay with me until your cousin gets back to town?"

"Wha…" Finn fumbled the teacup before it reached the nine o'clock position, nearly oversetting it. "You mean like at your home?"

Gary waggled his palm. "Not technically. My place isn't really… appropriate for guests, but I'm house-sitting for my friends, TD and Lonnie, and there's loads of room."

A place to stay. A place with *Gary*. Finn's belly tumbled, joy warring with apprehension, because in the past, whenever something seemed too good to be true, he got his ass kicked.

Or shot in the chest. Twice.

"Why? I might be, I don't know, an ax murderer or a cat burglar or something. I mean, I told you that my father's a criminal. You remember that, right? For all you know, I might be his protégé, groomed to carry on his legacy."

Gary tilted his head, a smile quivering on his lips. "You don't strike me as particularly feline, so cat burgling is out, and I'm pretty sure an ax murderer would need an ax." He made a show of peering under the table at Finn's pack. "You got an ax in there?"

Finn choked on a laugh. "No. Just clothes in serious need of a wash."

"And the way you talked about your father? Well, trust me, I've had *loads* of experience scoping out shady characters, and my instincts say you're not the evil mastermind type." He waggled a finger at Finn's chest. "Too much heart. Besides, remember what I said about flipping the script? Let's flip yours and see what happens."

"I don't know what to say. I mean, you have no reason to be so generous."

Gary stood. "I benefited enormously from somebody else's generosity. In my small way, I'm just paying it forward." Something flickered across his face. "Although, now that I think of it... How do you feel about dogs?"

Dogs? Seriously? Finn was surprised into a laugh which could almost qualify as a bark.

"Me and dogs, we're like this." He held up two fingers, pressed together. There was actually a pretty significant distance between weres and ordinary canines, but many in the supe community—vampires, for instance, who had a bug up their asses about shifters in general—didn't make the distinction.

"They're, um, *big*. And there are three of them."

"No problem."

"They'll have to approve you." Gary winced, rubbing his palms along the outside of his *extremely* well-fitting black jeans. "They're pretty protective of the house, so if they object, you won't be able to stay."

Finn grinned, because really, dogs? He could handle dogs. "I'm sure we'll get along fine."

Gary squinted, the picture of skepticism. "I appreciate your confidence, but these are really *unusual* animals." He tucked his thumbs in his pockets, smiling once more. "But don't worry. If they switch into full-on guard mode, we'll find another solution. It's just for a week, right? Just until your cousin gets back?"

"Right. A week." Finn fought to keep his grin in place, tough to do when he had to swallow around a lump in his throat. Gary wasn't offering him *forever*, just a temporary safety net. "Thank you. That would be great. Really."

Gary nodded decisively. "Excellent. We've got a plan then." He unhooked one thumb from his pocket and jerked it toward the door. "Let's go."

Finn gaped. "What? Now?"

"Why not? You don't have anywhere else to go today, do you?"

*I don't have anywhere else to go* ever. "No."

"As much as I love it when you hang out here in the bakery, it can't be comfortable. Provided the dogs are amenable, I'll get you settled, and you can relax until I get home this evening. We'll have dinner. Maybe watch a movie together." Gary bit his lip, uncertainty clouding his face. "If that's okay?"

"Are you kidding?" Finn grabbed his pack and surged out of his chair. "It's perfect."

"Melina," Gary called, "can you hold down the fort for a bit?"

She grinned, straightening up from where she'd been transferring fresh scones into the pastry case. "You *do* have employees, Gary. You don't have to be here every minute."

Gary huffed. "Yes, I have employees, but I don't want to *exploit* them."

She made shooing motions with both hands. "Go. Peyton and I have got this."

Gary fluttered his eyelashes at her. "How smart was I to hire such exceptional people?"

"Brilliant. Now get out of here."

Finn smiled at Melina as he followed Gary to the door. "Thanks, Melina."

"It's a pleasure." As the bell tinkled, she called, "Don't hurry back!"

Out on the sidewalk, Gary nodded to their left. "It's this way. I don't have a car, but it's just a couple of blocks, so an easy walk."

"I'm used to walking." With Gary at his side, Finn was hard pressed not to skip.

"Sorry about, um, Melina's comments. She and Peyton have kind of been trying to set us up for months."

Finn's loose trainer sole caught on the sidewalk and he stumbled. Only Gary grabbing his biceps to steady him kept him from face-planting on the concrete. "Really?"

Gary bit his lip, gazing up at Finn from under his lashes. "Yeah." He started to draw his hand away from Finn's arm. "If that makes you uncomfortable—"

"No!" Finn laid his own hand over Gary's, the jolt of their first skin-on-skin contact zinging straight to his heart. "I've been crushing on you since the first time I walked into the bakery."

Gary's smile had a *definite* playful edge. "Then why didn't you make a move?"

"Why didn't you?" Finn countered.

"I, um, have some issues with intimacy." He gave Finn's arm a squeeze and then withdrew his hand and resumed walking. "Besides, I want the bakery to be a safe space, somewhere nobody needs to worry about inappropriate behavior, somewhere everybody can be themselves."

"Ah. That's fair." Finn waited until they'd crossed the street and headed into a more residential area. "But you don't need to worry that I'll ask you for anything you're not willing to give, especially since *I've* got so little to offer. I mean, I told you about my situation. I'm broke. My father's an entitled, narcissistic psychopath—"

"You didn't say he was a psychopath!"

Finn slowed, gazing down at Gary. "Sorry. If that means you'd rather not have me staying with you—"

"Are you kidding? That makes me even more determined. Honey, you're a victim here too, and if there's one thing I know about, it's what it means to be victimized by entitled narcissists who, if they haven't stepped over the psychopath line, are definitely in sociopath territory." He stopped in front of a sprawling one-story house with mid-century vibes. "Here we are."

Finn blinked. *Holy shit.* A house this wide was a definite anomaly in this part of Portland, where builders were more likely to go up than out in order to squeeze in as many lots as possible on the available land.

Two long, brown-shingled wings swept back in a subtle V from the front door, which was painted a mellow pumpkin orange and had three circular windows in graduated sizes, the largest one centered at head height and the other two in a curve to the right, making it look as though bubbles were rising from the doorknob. Big picture windows flanked the door, one offering a glimpse of a brass-toned chandelier that looked like a model of the solar system.

"Wow."

"I know, right?" Gary smiled up at Finn. "The house belonged to TD's parents. He grew up here but moved away for work and it didn't come back to him until they'd already passed."

Finn winced. "Sorry for his loss."

"He's handling it, especially now that he's got Lonnie by his side." Gary sighed dreamily. "Those two are so perfect for each other." Then he shook his head, expression turning serious. "All right. Let's do this. The dogs are inside. Why don't we go around into the backyard before I introduce you? Then it'll be easier for you to escape through the gate if they react badly."

"Sounds fine to me."

Gary led the way around the left-hand wing to an extremely sturdy gate at least two feet taller than Finn's six feet. When they stepped through, Finn stumbled to a halt.

"*Wow.*"

The yard was deep and even wider than the house, populated with mature trees, well-maintained bushes, and beds of flowers that rivaled pictures Finn had seen of Monet's garden. A green and white striped hammock swayed gently in the breeze between two maples.

Gary chuckled. "Amazing, right? It's like they've got their own little park."

"Hells," Finn said, "I could live *here*, never mind the house." Dryads couldn't have done a better job with the place.

"I don't think you need to rough it that much."

Finn forbore from saying that he'd roughed it a lot more, and within the last twenty-four hours. He peered around the sun-dappled yard. It was pretty damn pristine for a house with three large dogs. They were either extremely well-trained or Gary's perspective on what constituted *large* wasn't the same as Finn's.

But then, weres were larger than actual wolves. Larger than any canine species too, with the possible exception of the Cwn Annwn, Herne the Hunter's pack of hellhounds.

"I'll let the dogs—" Gary's phone jangled from his pocket and he winced. "Sorry. I've got to check it. Melina or Peyton might need me."

"No worries. Take care of your business. I can wait."

Gary pulled his phone out, his eyes widening when he checked the screen, although whether with excitement or dread, Finn couldn't tell.

"I really have to take this. Do you mind waiting out here for a few minutes?" He was already backing away, lifting the phone to his ear as he fumbled a set of keys out of his pocket to unlock the sliding glass door. "I'll bring the pups out with me when I'm done with the call."

"No problem. I'll just"—the door closed behind Gary, cutting off his *Hello?* mid-word—"wait out here, I guess."

Not that it was a hardship. The big yard with its high, sturdy fence filled Finn with more peace than he'd felt... well... ever. His were hearing picked out a faint trickle of water. *Rear corner, two o'clock.*

Shit, all of this and a fountain too? How could he resist? He set his pack down on the flagstoned patio and wandered along a neatly trimmed grass path that wound between an herb garden—sage, mint, rosemary, thyme, and basil, according to Finn's nose—and a flower bed that was a riot of color and humming with bees.

Sure enough, tucked behind a stand of birch trees at the rear of the property was a... Well, not a fountain. A water feature. The little pool, surrounded by a tumble of white rocks ranging from the size of Finn's head to monsters five feet across, looked so natural that it seemed the house and yard might have grown up around it. Water flowed over the side of the tallest boulder, dancing from stone to stone before dropping into the amazingly clear pool, sending ripples to the feet of the statue of a small, big-eyed figure crouching to peer at its reflection.

Finn looked more closely at the statue, its surface sparkling where the sun caught flecks of quartz in the granite. He was surprised into a laugh because he recognized the figure as a character from a long-ago children's book. He'd always suspected the author must have seen a bauchan at some point, because the illustration had been a dead ringer.

The bushes rustled behind him. "Gary, is this Wishful from Emmaline Dalton's *Wishful Thinking*? I loved that book when I was a kid." Finn straightened, a smile on his face. "In fact, I think I learned to read with..." His smile died, because when he turned, it wasn't Gary blocking the path to the house.

*Fuck.* Gary hadn't been exaggerating when he told Finn the dogs were large. In fact, he might have been underplaying. Because the three hounds facing him easily topped Finn's waist, their square muzzled heads larger than his own, their muscled chests at least as wide as his.

"Shit," he muttered.

And they charged.

# Chapter Six

"Nectar & Ambrosia. This is Gan— Gary. How may I help you?"

"Gary, hello." The voice on the other end of the call was light and warm, yet somehow businesslike. "This is Del. I believe Peyton told you I'd be contacting you about a cake for my wedding."

"Yes." Embarrassingly enough, Gany's voice squeaked on the word. He cleared his throat. "Yes. He did."

Del sighed. "I'm very sorry—"

"Oh." Gany's heart plummeted. "You don't need the cake after all. That's perfectly fine. I appreciate the opportunity to—"

"No, no. That's not it at all. I do need the cake. Very much indeed. However, I can't tell you why, and I have to swear you to the utmost secrecy. Nobody can know about the cake, not even my fiancée. Is that something you can guarantee?"

Gany considered it. "Does the secrecy apply after the cake is served?"

"Of course not. I would never let anyone else take credit for your artistry. Once the cake is revealed and cut, everyone will know who's responsible. I promise you that."

Del's voice rang with an unusual resonance, almost like Cassandra's whenever she made one of her predictions— which none of the stupid Greeks had *ever* listened to. Well, Gany wasn't that clueless. He took Del at their word. But he couldn't pass up the opportunity for a little upselling— and maybe grabbing a benefit for Finn, too.

"Do you need servers? I could bring someone else with me to assist."

"Ah." A beat of silence. "It appears that would be necessary. So yes, please, but you'll need only one other."

"I have just the person."

Gany suspected that if he offered to simply *give* Finn money—which Gany had more than enough of, thanks to the Fates' settlement—Finn would refuse. Or if he didn't refuse, it would have dealt another blow to his pride, and Gany had no desire to beat him down any further.

But if he were to pay Finn for *working* for him, that would be another situation entirely.

"You know, Del, while the storefront for Nectar & Ambrosia is a bakery, my catering business isn't just baked goods. If you need hors d'oeuvres, soups, salads, or entrees, I'm happy to discuss menu options with you."

Del's chuckle was gentle and not in the least mocking. "I appreciate that. It won't be necessary for this event, but if all goes well, and if the reaction to your cake is as positive as Peyton assures me it will be, you'll have clients lining up. Wildwood, the venue where the wedding is taking place, is a relatively new resort, but it's already extremely popular. If you make a good impression on the owners, I'm sure you'll have more opportunities to work with them. Plus, they'll recommend you to friends and acquaintances, as will I. So what do you say? Will you do it?"

"We haven't discussed price."

"You're right. How does this sound?" Del named a price for the cake itself and for the service that made Gany blink. "That's what the other caterer is charging, but if it's too low—"

"N-n-no, no. That's perfect."

"Excellent. We have a deal then. The wedding is on Saturday, ten o'clock in the morning, at Wildwood. I'll email you the directions and the contact information for resort administration so you can sort out the details with them."

"Yes. Thank you." Gany was practically bouncing on his toes. "And may I offer you and your partner best wishes on your approaching marriage?"

"You may. Thank you." Del chuckled again, and Gany detected a rueful note. "I never saw this for myself, but she is the most remarkable person I have ever met. If you have any questions that Peyton or the resort can't answer for you, you may call me, although I may not be able to respond at once. My job keeps me rather busy at this time of year."

"Of course. Thank you. I'll— Thank you."

When Del ended the call, Gany couldn't resist kicking his shoes off and dancing around the living room. This was what he'd been hoping for. An *opportunity*. A chance to show what he could do, what he could offer. He knew that once people tasted his food, it would sell itself, and couple that with the kind of service that the freaking *cupbearer to the gods* could provide?

He was going to *crush* this!

Chest heaving, he finally stilled after a leap onto the sofa. He didn't feel bad about dancing on the furniture—his two bare feet made far less of an impression than twelve massive dog paws.

Dog paws.

Cerberus.

*Finn.*

"Hades!"

He scrambled off the cushions. "Sir? Bear?" He hopped from one foot to the other as he pulled his shoes back on. "Ozzie?"

The house was ominously quiet. TD had said the dogs were inside, hadn't he? Or at least implied when he'd talked about puppy-proofing the place. If that was wrong, if they'd been outside with Finn all this time while Gany had been trying to freaking *upsell* a catering job, and they'd *hurt* him...

He raced to the door and flung it open. "Finn!" he called. "Finn? Are you okay?"

Finn didn't answer, but he heard yips and whines and... was that a growl? Gany's heart tried to crawl out his throat. He ran across the patio, peering through the foliage. Priapus's balls, why was this yard so *big* and why were there so many *plants*? He couldn't see a damn thing.

He tried to whistle, but he'd never been good at it, and his lips were so numb right now that nothing but a feeble *phhht* emerged. "Ozzie! Bear! Come here at once. Sir, you too."

The dogs didn't respond, but bushes thrashed in the corner near the fountain, followed by another sharp yip. Gany barreled toward the sound, and when he rounded a massive rhododendron, Finn was *there*, sitting on the ground, his hair tousled and his shirt rucked up on one side.

"Finn!" Gany dove for him, flinging his arms around his neck and knocking him flat on his back, attempting to shield Finn's larger body with his own.

He clenched his eyes shut, waiting for the dogs to charge. But nothing happened. He cracked an eye open and met Finn's gaze.

"Hullo," Finn said, his voice hoarse and his smile crooked.

His arms came around Gany's back and *oh*, had anything ever felt so right? Warm and solid and *safe*, just as Gany had known it would be from the first time he'd met those sad hazel eyes on the bakery's opening day.

"Are you okay?" Gany ran his hands over Finn's face, along his throat, across his shoulders. "The dogs—"

"Hey." Finn captured Gany's hand, his grip loose and gentle, and pressed it against his cheek. "I'm fine."

"I'm so sorry. I thought the dogs were inside, and I..." Gany's voice died when he realized all three dogs were standing shoulder to shoulder just beyond Finn's head, staring down at both of the men with bottomless black eyes. "Finn. Be very, very still. I'm going to get off of you now and lure them away."

"Don't move on my account. I'm perfectly happy for us to stay right here," Finn said, his smile growing. He tilted his chin up until he was peering at the dogs upside down. "Heh. From this angle, the way they're standing makes them look like one dog with three heads."

Gany's smile was probably more of a grimace. "Imagine that."

All three dogs dipped their muzzles, and Gany flinched, sure that they were about to take a bite out of Finn, but instead, in perfect synchronization, like a canine rhythmic gymnastics squad, they each dropped a drool-soggy tennis ball and sat, tongues lolling.

Finn chuckled. "Okay, guys. We'll play again in a bit." He lifted one arm and made a downward patting gesture. "Down," he said in a low, commanding voice.

And amazingly enough, the dogs laid down in that classic Sphinx pose, their front paws stretched out and their ears perked.

"How did you do that?" Gany asked, wonderingly. "They don't even behave that well for Lonnie and TD."

"I've got experience with canines." Finn shrugged, the movement nestling Gany against his chest. "The guys and I reached an understanding." He stroked Gany's cheek. "I'd, um, like to reach an understanding with you, too."

Gany arched an eyebrow. "Is that so? What kind of understanding?"

"You mentioned before that you have issues with intimacy, so I don't want to overstep, but, well, here we are."

"Yes." Gany laughed weakly. "We certainly are."

"Are you uncomfortable?"

Gany bit his lip and ran through the mental exercises Dr. Kendrick had given him as part of his therapy. Finn hadn't forced any unwanted physical contact. *Gany* was the one who'd done that. "Actually, I'm not. Uncomfortable. At all. That is, if *you're* not."

"Like I said, I'm happy to stay right here. Although..." His gaze dropped to Gany's mouth. "I was wondering, since we're here and all. Would it be okay to... to kiss you?"

"Hmmm." Would it? Gany's middle sparked and quaked as he tried to balance between this unexpected—although not unwelcome—desire and deep-seated dread.

But then, Zeus had never *asked*. And Zeus's kisses were more like being mauled by a cross between a hydra, a kraken, and the old iteration of Cerberus—too many heads, too many arms, and *way* too much drool and tongue and hot, fetid breath.

After that horror, Gany had never had the least inclination to snog with any of the other gods, either. Dionysus always tried every year during the Dionysian revels. Aphrodite sideswiped him once, although he'd always thought it was pretty half-hearted, more as though it was expected, part of her usual routine. When he'd turned his face at the last minute and it had landed on his chin, she hadn't tried again. Apollo always tried to kiss everyone, but he'd avoided Gany after Leucates took a swan dive off a cliff rather than submit to Apollo's attentions.

Gazing into Finn's hopeful eyes, though, desire, coupled with hope, climbed over that trauma. Dr. Kendrick always told Gany he didn't have to comply with anybody's emotional timetable but his own. Maybe he'd reached the point—maybe he was finally *ready*—to find out what it was like to kiss someone by his own choice.

"That depends," he said.

Finn's expression turned wary. "On what?"

"On whether it's okay for *me* to kiss *you*."

"Mutual kiss understanding is a definite *hells yeah* from me."

"It's a yes for me too, but I should warn you—my past experience hasn't been the best, so I may not know exactly how to approach this."

Finn's crooked smile was back, and Gany could *totally* imagine pressing his own mouth against that little upturn of his lips, maybe for the rest of time. "If you're looking for a place to practice, then I volunteer as tribute."

Gany shuddered, visions of Iphigenia and too many other unwilling sacrifices to count dancing in his mind. "Not tribute, please. That makes it sound like you're just *enduring* the torture."

"Trust me, Gary." Finn's thumb stroked a fiery path along Gany's cheekbone, igniting something deep in the pit of his stomach, stirring something *below* that, too. "This is a dream come true for me. But I don't want you to feel like you're being pressured or—"

"No!" Gany lifted a shaky hand and brushed Finn's hair off his forehead. "I don't feel that at all."

Finn searched his face, gaze intent. "You're sure?"

"Absolutely." Gany hadn't gone through months of twice-weekly therapy with a psychologist so handsome he could give the gods a dash for their ducats without making real progress. Being in control of his body, his life, his choices—that made all the difference.

"Okay then. If you're ready, here goes."

Finn lifted his head and fitted his lips against Gany's, and *oh*.

Gany's heart fluttered and then *bloomed*, opening in a swell of warmth that filled his chest and... and... *other* places, too.

Finn's mouth was soft, his lips plush, his kiss gentle. *Respectful*. Giving, not taking. Inviting, not demanding.

And Gany wanted to accept that invitation because he knew, down in the most secret places in his heart, that if he wanted to say *no*, or *not this*, or *not yet*, that he could.

Gany whimpered, just a thread of sound, barely voiced, but somehow Finn heard it because he pulled back, peering up at Gany with worried eyes.

"Is this all right? It's not too much?"

"Totally all right, and not too much." Gany's gaze dropped to Finn's mouth. "Maybe not enough. Could you... do it again? For science?"

The worry in Finn's eyes vanished, and he grinned. "Science, huh? Well, you're a fan of flipping the script, so why don't you try it this time?"

"But I don't know how!"

"You know enough." Finn touched Gany's lips. "You've got your first experiment in the can, and trust me, you totally nailed it. You're welcome to repeat the process to see if you get the same results, or test another hypothesis and see what happens. Believe me, I'm happy to be your test subject—or rather, your lab partner. I'd welcome your mouth anywhere on my body."

Gany nipped Finn's finger. "Anywhere?"

Something hotter kindled in Finn's gaze. "Anywhere."

"Let's start here." Gany lowered his head and followed the elegant double swoop of Finn's eyebrows with a trail of tiny kisses, like butterflies playing hopscotch. He was rewarded with Finn's quick intake of breath and the subtle shift in his hips.

"Th-that's a good start," Finn croaked.

"I liked your lips on mine, though. I think we should conduct that experiment again." Gany wrinkled his nose. "Ugh, let's leave the science metaphors and go with something I know more about. This is like baking, right? We can test and taste. If we find a flavor we like, we can make it over and over."

"Over and over, huh?"

"Yes. We could *gorge* ourselves, but just because we like one recipe, doesn't mean we can't try others. We might find one that we like just as well, or even better."

"Yeah?" Finn cradled Gany's face between his palms. "What would you call our first dish, then?"

"Hmmm." Gany pretended to consider. "I'd call it... an amuse-bouche."

Finn chuckled. "Your *bouche* does more than *amuse*, Gary, and I'd be happy to keep *amusing* all night if you wanted."

Gany shivered, but not from alarm or aversion. *All night* sounded *wonderful*. But that warmth blooming inside him had turned into an *itch*, or maybe a smoldering fire that needed something to feed its flames.

"Could you"—Gany met Finn's gaze—"move on to an appetizer?"

Finn's eyes positively glowed—it must be the sun through the leaves overhead—and he grinned. "Something that lasts a little longer, you mean, that lingers on the tongue? A treat to savor?"

"Yes." Gany nodded, his curls bouncing. "That."

"All right, then. Here's the chef's special of the day."

Finn gently angled Gany's head, tilted his own the opposite way, and fitted their mouths together.

*Oh. This.* The little flame in Gany's chest flared brighter. Finn's lips were slightly parted, so Gany matched them, sharing breath, and when the tip of Finn's tongue flickered against Gany's lips? *Well.* He might not have a lot of kissing experience, but he knew how to RSVP to *that* invitation.

He opened wider and let Finn in.

# Chapter Seven

*Fuck, he tastes incredible.*

Finn teased Gary's tongue with his own. Advance. Retreat. Approach. Invite.

And Gary got it, picking up Finn's cues and embellishing them, his fingers flexing in Finn's curls, tilting his head for a better angle, a fuller taste, a deeper dive.

Gary was making surprised and appreciative sounds that he probably thought were inaudible, but that Finn's werewolf hearing picked up loud and clear. Gary didn't grind against him, but the hard length nestled against Finn's erection was a sign he was into this, at least as far as they'd gone.

But although Gary had *told* Finn that he had intimacy issues, he hadn't elaborated. Making out like this might be as much as Gary was ready for. And that was okay. That was all right. Because this right here—Gary flooding his senses with touch and taste and, Remus's *teeth*, smell— was more than okay and all right.

It was outstanding. Superlative. *Perfect.*

Finn was happy—no, ecstatic—to let Gary set their pace, to *give* whatever Gary asked.

But he refused to *take*, not when he had nothing to offer in return, when he might be gone by next week, when he'd be tarred with his father's crimes forever.

Finn couldn't do that to Gary. He wouldn't.

Then there was the little matter of Gary being human. A relationship between a human and a werewolf would send the supe council into the stratosphere.

Kissing, though. Kissing he could do. Kissing he could —

Gary pulled away with a gasp. "Gods, Finn."

"Yeah?" Finn was having a hard time catching his own breath. "You okay?"

"Okay? I'm... I'm... Sorry, I don't have *words*. I never thought it could feel like *this*." Gary bit his lip. "But—"

"I know." Finn tore his gaze away, not wanting to see regret chase the glow of wonder from Gary's face. "It's just a onetime thing."

"What? No! That is, I hope it's not. But there are three dogs staring at us." He lowered his head and murmured, "They *know*, Finn."

Finn's laugh escaped, shaking his chest and bouncing Gary enough that Finn had to steady him with both hands on the small of his back.

"They're just dogs, Gary, not psychics." He tilted his head to peer at the dogs upside down. "Although canines in general have boundary issues, and I've gotta admit, these guys look a little too interested in the proceedings for my comfort. I'd rather continue this in private." He gazed up at Gary. "If you, that is... Do you want to? Do this? Try any more, um, recipes?"

"I already said this isn't a onetime thing, Finn. Not for me. I—" His eyes popped wide and he pushed himself to his knees, straddling Finn's thighs. "Oh gods, I almost forgot." His smile went nuclear. "That call! I've got a job!"

Finn sat up and rested his hands on Gary's waist. "I know. The bakery—"

"Yes, yes. But I've been trying to launch a catering business, and every single bid I've submitted has been turned down."

"Every one? How many are we talking about?"

Gary bit his lip. "Maybe... twenty?"

"Twenty? You're joking. Have they *tasted* your food?"

Gary's cheeks went adorably pink. "Yes, but there are other factors people consider when booking a caterer. One of them is reviews from past clients, and I don't have any." His expression darkened. "At least none that I'd trust to talk to any humans."

Finn's brows drew together. "Humans?"

"I mean, you know, *people*." He grabbed Finn's hands, his grip almost too tight in his obvious excitement. "But this job? I didn't even have to submit a bid. *They* came to *me*, through a referral from Peyton, and they're paying me more than I'd have dared ask." His gaze drifted up, his smile dreamy. "My first wedding cake."

"That's amazing." Finn dropped a kiss on Gary's forehead. "Congratulations."

Gary peeked up at Finn from under his lashes. "That's not all. They'll need a server to assist me. And I was wondering... Could I hire you?"

Finn's breath hitched. *A job. A paycheck. A chance I could survive without begging Tanner for money.* The weight on his shoulders lessened for an instant before it slammed back down, heavier than before. He slid his hands free from Gary's grasp.

"Is this some kind of pity hire?"

"Pity? Seriously?" Gary narrowed his eyes, leaning forward to point at Finn's nose. "Pity is the *last* thing on my mind when I think about you, especially when we just mauled each other in front of Cerber— and Ozzie. But *need* is another thing. I need someone to help me."

He lifted his palms between them. An invitation. Finn sighed—*no pride anymore, remember?*—and took the offer, fitting his hands over Gary's.

"Okay, I'm listening. Tell me about it."

"Melina and Peyton will have to run the bakery while I'm away, and probably while I'm trying to get the cake recipe right, so they won't have the bandwidth to do much more. You need a job. The money is coming from the client, *specifically* for a server. It's a win-win, Finn." Gary bounced a little on Finn's thighs—*distracting... gah!*—and pumped a fist, grinning up at the sky. "Take that, Homer! I'm a poet too!"

Finn had to laugh at Gary's clear joy. Besides, if he were honest with himself, that knee-jerk reaction, that inclination to refuse, was rooted in a life that was no longer his. As his father's son, privileged within the pack, he'd have considered this kind of work beneath him.

No, scratch that. His *father* would have considered the work beneath *his son*.

If Finn didn't want to be his father's son anymore—and he most definitely did not—he needed to leave those attitudes and values in the past.

*Don't live for him anymore. Live for myself.*

And maybe—if he were very lucky—he could live *with* someone else, could *share* a life with someone like Gary, whose light could brighten even Finn's shadowed soul.

"All right. I'll do it, but—"

"Yay!" Gary flung himself at Finn, wrapping his arms around his neck and kissing him soundly on the mouth. "Thank you."

"I'm the one who should be thanking you. And I do. But don't I need some kind of license to do this?"

Gary half-shrugged and stood, holding out a hand to draw Finn to his feet too. "You'll need a food-handler's license, but you have thirty days to take the exam. If you like the work, maybe..." He bit his lip again. "Do you think you might consider working with me more? If this takes off the way the client thinks, I'll have enough work that I'll need more help, both in the bakery and in the catering side hustle. We can use this as a test case. To see how well we work together and whether it's something you'd like to pursue." Another coy look from under his lashes. "While we pursue *other* things, too. I have a lot of... *recipes* I'd like for us to test."

"I'd like that." He smiled down at Gary, feeling lighter than any time in the last year or more. "When do we start?"

Gary's flirtatious expression vanished, replaced with obvious whites-around-the-eyes panic. "Oh, gods. The ceremony's on *Saturday*." He clutched the front of Finn's shirt. "I only have *two days*—no, a day and a half because it's got to be noon, right? A day and a half to figure out how to make a wedding cake."

"You've never done one before?"

Gary shook his head. "There's never been a call for anything over three layers at the bakery. This one—gods, Finn. Eight tiers!"

"In that case, we'd better get to work." He laid his hands over Gary's, holding them against his chest. "I may not have bakery experience, but I can be your manual labor. I'll do the grunt work while you make your magic." He moved their joined hands to his stomach. "And I'm more than happy to test any of your recipes." He peered down into Gary's face, smiling crookedly. "The ones involving cake or the ones that involve you and me."

Gary beamed at him. "You're the best."

"Hold that thought until I've actually done anything."

"Oh, you've already done *something*." Gary lifted onto his toes and kissed Finn softly. Then, his expression turning businesslike, he freed his hands and pulled his phone out of his back pocket. "I need to do some research," he said, typing furiously. "And I'll definitely need to shop for ingredients before we head back to the bakery."

"Why don't you head inside and put together your shopping list? I'll spend a little more time with the pups while you're getting organized, and we'll head out as soon as you've made your preparations. Sound cool?"

Gary gazed up at him, and the look in those dark, liquid eyes... *Oh.* Finn was pinned in place, helpless, but not the least sorry for it.

"Sounds perfect," Gary murmured. "I'll give you a call when I'm ready."

He headed for the house, glancing over his shoulder to smile at Finn every few steps.

"Look out!" Finn called, just in time to keep Gary from planting a foot in the herb garden.

Gary stumbled sideways, laughing. "Thanks." He gestured to the sliding glass door. "Since I've clearly surrendered any claim I ever had of being smooth, I'll have to settle for being marginally efficient."

Finn waited until Gary slid the door shut and vanished into the shadows inside the house before he turned to glare down at the dogs.

"We have things to do, guys. Important things. I can't spend all day throwing balls for you."

The three of them glanced at each other and then very deliberately—and totally in synch—placed their left front paw over their ball.

When they'd charged at him before, although Finn hadn't had time to shift, he'd freed his alpha potential. His father had never allowed it at home, but Finn had learned to control and respect the power when he was in Idaho for his Howling.

So he'd lowered his head, bared his teeth, growling low, eyes burning with the amber flare of alpha authority.

The dogs had been so astonished that they'd frozen in their tracks. After glancing at each other in bemusement, they'd uttered excited yips and rolled over, showing him their bellies and tilting their heads back to expose their throats.

Now, though, bright eyes fixed on him, they vibrated with barely contained energy. Gary's comment was right on the money, even though he'd been referring to something else.

They *knew*.

They knew precisely what he was, and they wanted to play, not with a human, but with their alpha. With their *canid* alpha.

"Fine, but only for a few minutes. Gary needs me, and not as a wolf."

Finn sighed as he stripped off his shirt and tossed it over a nearby tree branch. *I just hope I don't disappoint him.*

Shielded from the house and the neighbors by the birch trees, he let his shift take him, to the bouncing glee of the three pups, and hoped he hadn't just inadvertently formed a pack. Because not only was that a complication he didn't *need* right now.

It was a complication he couldn't afford.

# Chapter Eight

Gany couldn't help doing a little jig on his way to the kitchen. Those kisses... *swoon*. Finn was *delicious*. If Gany could capture that flavor, this *feeling* of lightness and brightness and rightness the flavor sparked? If he could distill it all somehow, infuse it in a pastry? People would be lined up around the block—twice—outside Nectar & Ambrosia every day.

*If I didn't snabble them all first.*

His steps slowed and he came to a stop in front of the fridge, his reflection blurred and distorted in the stainless steel.

Just as shadowy and indistinct as he was himself.

Gany wasn't even sure *what* he was anymore. Was he even still human? He was nearly four thousand years old. He ought to have been dust on a sheep-dotted hillside millennia ago. Now that he wasn't existing solely on nectar and ambrosia, the food that granted perfect health and eternal youth and immortality to the gods, would he begin aging normally?

If not, what did that mean to his friends? Melina, of course, knew who he was. But Peyton didn't. What would they think when Gany—if *Gary*—stayed looking the same, year after year, decade after decade?

Or worse, what if all his years started to catch up with him and he aged *faster* than everyone around him? Would he even *be able* to die? Or would he turn into a withered, dithering husk like Tithonus after Eos forgot the little matter of youth when she petitioned Zeus to give her lover immortality?

"Hades, I could be nothing but a cricket or cicada or some other irritating, noisy insect by the next solstice," he muttered.

The recipes for nectar and ambrosia were seared into his brain—that happened when you prepared the freaking stuff every day, century after century. Should he make more, keep it on hand just in case his joints started to creak or his vision go dim?

"I should have asked for more details before the Fates set us free," he grumbled as he yanked open the junk drawer and pulled out a pad and pen.

He took a deep breath and exhaled, closing his eyes to center himself. Whatever he was, whatever was going to happen down the road, next month, next year, next *century*, in two days—no, a day and a half—he had to have *the* perfect wedding cake ready to go.

He sat down at the counter, pen in hand, and started sketching. Del's email had included the flavors they'd opted for in their other cake, but had also said they wouldn't mind if Gany experimented a little with a couple of the layers, as long as at least one of them was lemon and at least one filling was raspberry. Decorations, though, were completely up to Gany.

What if he leaned in to his roots, to the Mediterranean slant he wanted to give the business? A honey cake layer with walnut filling? A deep chocolate olive oil layer flavored with almond? The raspberry filling would be fantastic with that. Maybe a light Italian sponge. That might work for the lemon layer, but how should he flavor the filling?

He wrinkled his nose. Not rose, no matter how pervasive it was in Middle Eastern desserts. No florals at all. He *loathed* them and avoided them in all his recipes, probably because Zeus's soap was heavily scented with lavender, although it was always undercut by the ever-present pong of Olympian spunk—a combination Gany *never* wanted to experience again.

Finn's scent was so different. He'd clearly bathed last with a rather harsh soap, but its harsh antiseptic echo didn't fully mask another, luscious scent, like forests and lakes and fresh breezes from the mountains. Firmly anchored in the earth, where Gany wanted to keep his own feet planted forever.

"Stop daydreaming about your crush," he ordered himself sternly, gripping the pen tighter. "There'll be time for more with him later."

He tapped the pen on the pad, once, twice, bearing down harder with each strike. *Would* they have time, though?

Gany's tempo increased, jabbing the paper faster and faster in keeping with his swirling thoughts and the knot in his middle. Yes, the dogs had accepted him, so Finn would be here for at least a week. But what then? Would Finn vanish into the sunset to cast himself on his cousin's mercy? What if his cousin didn't *have* any mercy? Would he stay here? Did Gany *want* him to stay? What would happen when TD and Lonnie came home?

Gany looked down at the pad to see that he'd defaced the cake sketch with dozens of tiny pits. "Oh, for the love of—"

The doorbell rang, and Gany fumbled the pen, dropping it on the floor at his feet. He picked it up, frowning. TD hadn't mentioned that he and Lonnie were expecting a delivery. Unless he had and Gany hadn't been paying attention, which wasn't entirely outside the realm of possibility.

The bell rang again, and he set the pen next to the pad and stood, peering into the backyard through the kitchen window. His view was limited from this angle, but he saw one of the pups—not that he could tell the difference unless they were standing together, since Sir was always on stage left, Bear in the middle, and Ozzie on the right—dash past, clearly unconcerned about whoever was on the doorstep.

The bell rang a third time, in an elongated jangle, as though the visitor had grown impatient and leaned on the buzzer. Gany hesitated, biting his lip. It should be fine. It was probably fine.

Oh! TD had mentioned once that they had the dogs' food delivered regularly, so that's probably what this was, and since the dogs were the primary god deterrent, and they weren't reacting, the person at the door was clearly no threat.

Gany chuckled as he crossed the living room. "Not everything is about you, Ganymede."

Through the uppermost circular window, he could see a brown ball cap with an orange patch sporting the silhouettes of a dog and cat. Yep, dog food delivery. Had to be.

He pasted a smile on his face as he flipped the deadbolt and opened the door. "Hell—"

The woman on the porch, the cap pulled low over her brow, grabbed Gany's biceps and yanked him outside. "Ha! Got you first!"

Gany squinted into the bill's shadow. "Artemis? What are you—"

"Let go of him." Finn's voice almost reverberated in the air, deep and rough, like a velvet saw blade.

Artemis released him, although she looked just as surprised about it as Gany. She backed up a couple of steps, frowning at Finn, who stepped out the door and stood by Gany's side, a warm, solid, *reassuring* presence.

Finn angled his head toward Gany, but didn't take his gaze off Artemis. "Do you know this person?"

Gany folded his arms and glared at the goddess, who was wearing jeans, Birkenstocks, and a cropped green tank that revealed an opal navel ring. The orange patch on her hat bore the name of an animal rescue league, not the pet supply.

"I do. But she shouldn't be anywhere near this house."

"Restraining order, huh?" Finn said.

"Something like that. She's not allowed to cross the threshold."

"I didn't," Artemis said sulkily. "You came outside."

"I only came outside because you yanked me through the door." Gany rubbed his biceps. "And may I say... ow? I'd think you'd have learned your lesson about"—he glanced sidelong at Finn—"attacking men."

"I wasn't—"

"If you grabbed him without his consent," Finn said implacably, that burr of command still in his voice, "you attacked him. Now I think you'd better leave."

She bridled at that. "Who are you to give me orders, cur?"

Finn grinned, his teeth, glinting white in the sun, looked sharp and almost lethal. "I'm the guy with three really big guard dogs behind me."

He wrapped an arm around Gany's waist and moved them both aside to reveal Sir, Bear, and Ozzie, shoulder to shoulder again, fangs bared and slavering, growls vibrating in their throats, steadily gaining volume until they sounded like a trio of industrial stand mixers.

Artemis stumbled down the porch steps, but stopped in the middle of the flagstone path, glaring up at them. "Just you wait, Ganymede. You'll see. I'll beat them all to the top." She turned and stalked away, the ponytail tucked through her snapback swinging.

"Man," Finn said, "she's almost as buff as that guy from the bakery. Are all your friends this jacked?"

"They're not my friends," Gany mumbled. "They're pains in my ass."

"No shit." Finn shook his head. "Not if they can't even get your name right."

Gany buried a wince, but to sidestep the whole *Ganymede* issue, he turned to the dogs, who were now sitting side by side, tongues lolling, as they blocked the door. He propped his fists on his hips.

"And *you* are supposed to keep them out, or at least warn a guy."

All three dogs hung their heads and dropped, belly-crawling to cower behind Finn's legs—a neat trick, considering their size and that the porch wasn't *that* big.

"Shit," Finn said, running both hands through his hair, which, weirdly, seemed about an inch longer than it did when Gany left him in the yard twenty minutes ago. But that was ridiculous, so probably it had just escaped whatever product Finn used to keep his waves tamed. "I'm so sorry, Gary. I distracted them. We were playing in the backyard, and they got so involved in chasing m— the balls, that I don't even think they heard the doorbell."

Gany studied the dogs, frowning. The doorbell should have been irrelevant. They should have detected the presence of a god within a hundred yards. "Did you?"

"Did I what?"

"Hear the doorbell?"

Finn cleared his throat, rubbing the back of his neck. "It... Yeah, that was it."

Gany crossed his arms. "Finn."

Finn blew out a breath and let his hand fall to his side. "Okay, fine. I just felt like... you were afraid."

Gany blinked. "You did?"

"Yeah. It's... well, kind of a thing in my, er, family."

"Empathy?"

He brightened, almost as though he were grasping at an explanation that wasn't precisely true, but was at least believable. Gany knew all about that, since his earthside arrival required frequent misdirection and vaguesplaining, too.

"Yeah," Finn said. "Empathy. That."

While there was obviously more to it, Gany decided to let it pass for now as they all returned inside. Finn scowled as he threw the deadbolt, almost as though he were blaming the door for not keeping Gany safe.

That level of care was... disquieting. Nobody had ever tried to keep him safe, including his own father. Zeus hadn't been concerned with Gany's *safety*, and certainly not his happiness, only with his presence, because with Zeus, it was all about *possession*, not about consideration.

Disquieting but also... endearing, that Finn would worry about Gany's well-being when he clearly had his own raft of problems.

Finn laced his fingers with Gany's. "So. Got the cake deets nailed down?"

"Cake?" Gany's stomach jolted. "Gods! The cake." *That* was why he couldn't press Finn for more answers now. He had a *cake* to bake. In a day and a half.

He let go of Finn's hands and hurried over to the counter where he'd left his sketches and notes. He held up the pad. "What do you think?"

Finn studied it, head tilted to one side like one of the pups, and he scratched his nose. "Do those divots represent some kind of decoration?"

Gany glanced at the sketch, at the dents he'd jammed into the paper when he'd been stewing about his and Finn's future. "Oh. No. I was just, you know, brainstorming."

"I'm not so sure," Finn said slowly. He traced a path on the sketch with one finger. "It looks kind of like a bird. Or a flight of them. See?" He traced the path again and Gany's eyebrows rose. "Aren't doves a thing with weddings?"

"Not doves," Gany said, certainty settling in his middle. "A swan."

"Are swans wedding things too? I mean, I know they mate for life." He shivered. "I also know you do *not* want to get into a fight with one. Those wings are *lethal*."

"Speaking from experience?"

Finn smiled, a mischievous twinkle in his eyes. "No comment." He kissed Gany's forehead. "What's next?"

Gany gazed down at his sketch, and a vision of the finished cake rose, as crystal clear as though it physically floated in the air in front of him rather than in his imagination. Despite the cliché of a pair of swan necks forming the shape of a heart, he was visualizing a single swan. Her neck would twine around the top three layers, her wings wrap the bottom four, with her head hovering over the top layer in lieu of a cake topper, which, for some reason, felt wrong. But in her beak… *Yes!* A rainbow jewel.

The certainty that he'd got it right settled over him, and just like that, the flavors of sponge, fillings, and frosting solidified in his mind.

"Next, I need to practice." He bit his lip, smiling up at Finn. "I'll make the samples at the bakery so Melina and Peyton can weigh in on the results too. I've got enough flour and sugar and butter in the pantry there… I think. But if I have to run multiple tests—and if the final version doesn't work—I'll need more. I can't short the bakery. That's not fair to my loyal regulars."

"Do you have a local baker's supply?" Finn asked.

"Yes."

"Do they deliver?"

Gany scrunched up his nose. "Not with so little notice."

Finn's eyebrows bunched, his forehead wrinkling, and for some reason, the dogs looked up at him and whined.

He absently patted each of their heads and they leaned against him, sighing.

"I'd offer to run over and pick up your supplies, but there are a couple of problems with that. First, I wouldn't be able to pay—"

"Not a problem," Gany said, hope warming his middle. He grabbed the pad and flipped to a new page to jot down the address and his account number. "I'll call and let them know you've got authority to charge everything to my name. I'll give you some cash, too."

Finn's frown deepened. "Are you sure you should trust me with your financial details? You don't really know me."

Gany flicked his fingers at the dogs, whose eyes were all half-lidded in bliss. "I go by the pups. They trust you, and they literally trust *no one* except for TD, Lonnie, and me. If you're on their approved list, that's good enough for me."

"So," Finn said, disappointment flavoring his tone, "just the dogs' opinions?"

Gany edged closer, nudging Sir's head out of the way so he could wrap his arms around Finn's waist. "Mine, too. It's not like we only met five minutes ago. I've seen you every day for months, and you've never once done anything mean or rude or ungenerous. You're really trying to make peace with your cousin. I respect that."

In fact, it was so refreshing as to make Gany nearly giddy: someone who was serious about redemption, about atoning for his past mistakes. The gods were clearly not grasping the concept even now.

"Really?" Finn asked hopefully.

"Promise." Gany kissed him, soft but slow, because some things were worth savoring.

"Then there's the other thing." Finn rested his forehead against Gany's. "How do I get there? A ride share?"

"Oh!" Gany blinked. "Can you drive?"

Finn smiled wryly. "Depends on who you ask. My father would say no. I put a dent in his new Lincoln when I was learning, so he never let me get behind the wheel of one of the pa— one of our cars again. But I'm licensed and can drive perfectly well."

"Then let me make a list."

# Chapter Nine

As Finn pulled the borrowed Prius out of the bakery supply lot, its cargo space filled with enormous sacks of flour and three kinds of sugar, blocks of butter and chocolate—who knew you could buy the stuff in literal bricks?—jugs of honey, bags of walnuts, nubbly cardboard crates of eggs, and flats of raspberries, he actually found himself whistling Hunter's Moon's sprightly "Lover's Reel."

He barked a laugh. How long had it been since he'd been carefree enough to do that? Usually, if any music unreeled in his brain, it was heavy and grim, like "Song of the Volga Boatmen," or sharp and fatalistic like "O Fortuna," or else one of Hunter's Moon's old songs, all mournful and angsty, from when Gareth Kendrick was still obsessing over his lost love.

Now, though? He wanted *all* the upbeat anthems, the sappy love songs, the sweetness and light, because Gary *liked* him, liked him enough to kiss him. But more than that, Gary *trusted* him, even after Finn had spilled the tea about his less than stellar past behavior.

Not only that, he had a place to stay and a job. Yeah, maybe both were only temporary, but just yesterday, he hadn't had any hope at all of his life improving, let alone turning around so completely.

He alternated between whistling, humming, and singing at the top of his voice all the way to the bakery. Gary had told him to pull around to the back so they could load the supplies directly into the storeroom, so Finn navigated the one-way grid, passing the park—hey, maybe he could take the pups there later—and turned into the alley that led behind the line of stores.

The whistle died on his lips, because black smoke was pouring out an open door halfway down the alley. Shit, was that the bakery?

"No, no, no," he moaned. "Please, no."

Finn parked the Prius haphazardly and leaped out, not bothering to shut the door before racing down the alley.

As he got nearer, he could see the gold *Nectar & Ambrosia* lettering on the heavy door that stood ajar at the top of a concrete loading ramp. Fuck, the fire *was* in the bakery.

"Gary!" he shouted, vaulting over the ramp's metal rail, earning a lungful of smoke for his trouble. Coughing, he pulled the neck of his T-shirt up over his mouth. The smoke was so thick he could barely see. He dropped to his hands and knees, hoping the air would be clearer near the floor, and crept through the door.

Through the haze, he could see the metal legs of the prep tables, the toe kick under the cabinets, and the base of some hefty appliance, but no*body's* feet and—thank the gods—no crumpled bodies. He didn't see any flames, however, only smoke.

"Gary," he called again, although his throat closed on the word, making it more of a croak. "Gary, are you in here? Are you all right?"

"Finn!"

Finn's arms shook, elbows almost buckling from sheer relief. "Gary? Where are you?"

"I'm outside. For the love of the gods, get out of there!"

Steadying his arms, Finn choked and hacked his way back across the kitchen. The instant he breached the doorway, he sucked in a huge lungful of air, only to cough helplessly because the smoke followed him out, nearly as dense as it was inside.

Then a hand appeared through the haze and caught his arm, pulling him stumbling down the concrete ramp and into Gary's arms.

"You okay?" Finn wheezed.

Gary didn't answer, his full lips pressed in a tight line as he led Finn away and out of the alley. Tears were leaking down his cheeks, but since Finn's eyes were watering too, he wasn't sure whether it was smoke-related, or, you know, *smoke*-related.

The pavement in front of the bakery was empty, although the sidewalk directly across the street was crowded with milling people, some clutching Nectar & Ambrosia cups, and others just gawking at the spectacle of the dense black cloud hovering over the bakery like its own personal murderous mood.

"What happened?" Finn croaked, his throat burning and his nose stinging like he'd inhaled a handful of nettles. "And where's the fucking fire department?"

"They're on their way," Gary said, a catch in his own voice.

"They should be here now! The whole block could burn down!"

Gary laid his palm against Finn's heaving chest. "It's only been two minutes."

Finn blinked, eyebrows lifting. "Two minutes? But the smoke—"

"Yeah, I know. It started billowing out of the oven and set off the alarm. Melina got all the customers out safely, thank the Fates. I sent Peyton out right away to make the 9-1-1 call, but by the time I left, I hadn't seen any flames. Just smoke."

Gary's face crumpled, and Finn pulled him in against his chest.

"I'm so sorry, Gary."

"My bakery," Gary said, his voice muffled against Finn's shirt. "This was my dream, Finn."

"I know."

He kissed the top of Gary's head, the inky curls smelling like the acrid smoke—unless that was just Finn's nose. *Fucking werewolf senses.* He probably wouldn't be able to smell anything *but* smoke for a week.

"I'd been having trouble with inconsistent bakes this morning," Gary said with a sniffle, "but I never thought the oven was homicidal."

Sirens wailed from down the street, getting nearer, and a moment later, the red hook and ladder truck pulled up in front of the bakery, an ambulance and a police patrol car right behind it.

The police officers immediately started herding the onlookers farther away.

"For your own safety, if you'll move along?" one officer said to Finn and Gary.

"Please," Gary said. "That's my bakery. I need to tell the firefighters what I know."

The officer chewed on her lip for a second, but then gestured to a tall firefighter whose helmet read *Captain*. When he joined them, she said, "This is the business owner."

The man—who was a good head taller than Finn, who was a head taller than Gary—looked down at them out of intense amber eyes. "What can you tell me?"

"The commercial oven is the source of the smoke." Gary pointed down the alley. "The direct access door is there." He looked up with pleading eyes. "Please. I know you have to do what you have to do to keep people safe, but I didn't see any actual fire before I ran out. Don't"—his voice broke—"destroy anything you don't have to?"

The captain smiled down at Gary and, for an instant, Finn detected a different kind of smoke—something redolent of sun-baked sand and tamarisk and myrtle instead of the chemical-laden smoke from the kitchen.

"We'll only do what's necessary. I promise."

"Thank you." Gary nestled against Finn, and Finn gathered him close. "That's all I can ask."

The captain nodded and strode off, a gaggle of other firefighters in full turnout gear falling in behind him. Two firefighters stayed behind, hooking the hose up to the hydrant on the corner. Gary watched them, trembling against Finn, and Finn tried to keep his coughs buried in his chest.

"Do you think they'll have to use water?"

"I don't know, babe," Finn said, startled into a coughing fit when the endearment slipped out.

Gary frowned up at him. *Shit.* Had Finn just *assumed* they were on the same page? Did Gary want to keep distance between them?

But he was cuddled against Finn right now, in public, in full view of anyone with a cell phone, so it wasn't as though he objected to PDA. Maybe he just objected to being *claimed* that way without his consent?

"Sorry," Finn said. "That just slipped ou—" Another coughing fit racked his body and he had to turn away from Gary and brace his hands on his knees.

Gary's hand was warm on the small of his back. "Finn, I was frowning because you were coughing. You're clearly suffering from smoke inhalation." He leaned closer and chuckled. "Although if you think I object to you calling me *babe*, your brain might have been affected as much as your lungs."

Finn inhaled shakily—managing not to cough, thank fuck—and stood. "I'll be fine."

Gary's eyes narrowed. "Yes, you will. Because I'm taking you to the EMTs right now." He linked his elbow with Finn's and drew him into the street toward the ambulance.

Finn resisted. He couldn't risk human paramedics taking his vitals. Werewolves ran hot, and their calon—the extra organ every supe had under their heart—always created an echo that made human medical personnel order an EKG, stat. And don't get him started on blood pressure. If his cough persisted, he could go back to St. Stupid's and get treated there.

"I'll really be fine." Of course, he choked on the last word and started coughing again. Remus's balls, what was *in* that smoke?

"Sir?" The captain was suddenly there, in front of them, his face shield flipped up, and Finn gave thanks for the respite.

Gary gulped audibly, and he glanced at the firefighters with the hose. They were alert, but unmoving. "Yes?"

The captain smiled down at Gary. "I've got good news and bad news."

Gary closed his eyes for an instant, his hand tightening on Finn's, before he met the captain's gaze. "Give me the good first, so I can brace myself for the bad."

"The incident appears limited to the commercial oven alone. No sign of open flames, and no indication that other fixtures or the building itself were compromised in any way."

"That's…" Gary inhaled and exhaled shakily. "Good. I guess." He peered up at the captain. "The bad?"

"Although the oven didn't precisely catch fire, we can't identify why it's still smoking. There didn't seem to be anything in it?" He lifted his brows along with the end of his sentence.

"No. Not yet."

"As we thought. Which means the problem must be in its wiring. We'll need to dismantle it and remove it from the premises, in case there's an issue we can't detect now."

Gary nodded glumly as a pair of firefighters walked by, each carrying what was obviously an oven door. "I understand."

"There'll also be significant smoke damage to the kitchen. It didn't seem to spread to the restaurant, but I'm afraid you'll need to discard any exposed foodstuffs."

Again, Gary nodded as two more firefighters walked past, carrying a charred metal panel between them.

"Now," the captain said, a note of command in his tone as he beckoned to a tall woman in an EMT uniform, "anyone who was in that kitchen needs to be checked out. That smoke was quite caustic. It could have severe effects if you inhaled enough of it."

Gary ignored the EMT. "Do you know when I'll be able to get back inside?"

"Give your contact information to the officers. We'll be in touch."

With a final nod, he turned and strode back toward the kitchen, where his team was wrestling more pieces of Gary's oven out the door.

"Well," Gary said tartly, "*that* wasn't precisely informative."

The EMT, whose name—M. Courtland—was embroidered on her shirt, chuckled. "That's because he doesn't know. Now, my partner's already cleared your co-worker... Peyton, is it?"

Gary tensed. "They're okay then? I thought they'd left before the smoke got too bad, but *any* of that smoke was too much."

"They're fine." She chuckled. "And feeling good enough to flirt with my partner."

Gary winced, squinting one eye. "Do I need to apologize for my employee's behavior?"

"Nah," she said. "It's just what the grumpy cuss needs." She leaned forward. "I actually saw him smile, which hasn't happened since the premier of *Strange New Worlds*. But like I said, Peyton's fine. You two need to be checked out as well, though."

"She's right." Finn pushed Gary forward. "You go."

Gary propped his fists on his hips and glared up at Finn. "*I'm* not the one who's hacking up a lung in the middle of the street."

"I'm no—" Another coughing fit prevented Finn from lying outright. Once he caught his breath, he narrowed his eyes. He glanced at Courtland. "You said you've got a partner, right?" At her nod, he met Gary's glare with one of his own. "I'll go if you go."

Gary heaved a sigh loaded with exasperation and long-suffering. "Fine."

"Okay, then. I'll—" He coughed again and Gary pushed him forward.

Courtland took Finn's arm and grinned at Gary. "Don't worry. I'll take good care of him."

# Chapter Ten

"Let's go."

Gany didn't bother to look around at the gruff order, even when the speaker took his arm, his gaze fixed on Finn as Courtland all but frog-marched him down the street.

As he was led away, Gany kept his attention fixed on Finn until he was seated on the back of the open ambulance.

*Wait a minute.*

If the ambulance was over *there*, getting farther away with every stumbling step as Courtland's grumpy partner hauled Gany along in his wake, then…

He dug in his heels and finally looked around. The tall, broad-shouldered figure in the blue EMT uniform who was towing him along the sidewalk had a *very* familiar halo of gold-tipped black curls.

"Apollo," Gany hissed. "What in hades are *you* doing here?"

The ersatz EMT glanced back irritably, and yep, it really was Apollo. The sun god's unmistakable high-bridged nose made it extra easy for him to look down it at those beneath him—which, as far as he was concerned, was everybody, especially Gany.

"Don't cause a scene, Ganymede. Just come on."

"Don't cause a *scene*? This is the second time today one of you lousy Olympians has tried to grab me."

Apollo smirked at Gany with his stupid, perfect face. "I think not."

"No? Your *sister* showed up at TD and Lonnie's place, expressly against the terms of your plea deal with the Fates, and almost yanked me off my feet."

A frown marred his wide brow. "I wasn't disagreeing about the grab, only about the count. She wasn't the first and I'm not the second."

Gany frowned. "You mean Eros?"

Apollo's square jaw tightened. "Eros was here? Damn. I didn't think he'd move that fast."

"If he wasn't the first, who was? Nobody else has tried…"

His mouth dried. Surely not *Finn*. The gods, especially Zeus, were notorious for disguising themselves to get their rocks off, but Finn wasn't… He couldn't be… Gany would have been able to *tell*, if not sometime during the months of flirting and pining, then today, when they'd finally kissed.

No god had ever kissed as well as Finn.

Apollo jerked his head at the bakery, which still had a cloud of smoke hovering over its roof. "No?"

Gany's jaw dropped. "My *oven*? That was *intentional*? One of you did that on *purpose*? You could have *killed* someone!" *Finn.* Gany glanced back at the ambulance. Finn wasn't there anymore.

"Well, we had to do *something* to get you out of there," Apollo said testily. "We're not allowed to go inside the damned place, any more than we're allowed in TD's house."

"What did you *do*?"

He shrugged. "Wasn't me. Hephaestus arranged it. Modified one of Zeus's lightning bolts and shot it into the oven from outside the building. So he's not technically in violation of the rules." Apollo's brow darkened. "Bloody irritating, though. If Artemis had done the job right, we wouldn't have to split the points three ways."

"Points? What— Oh, for the Fates' sake. Is this about that stupid app?"

Apollo's face took on a shifty expression worthy of Hermes. "It's not stupid."

"No?" Gany gestured to Apollo in his uniform. "Are you even an EMT?"

He jutted his chin out. "I could be. I *invented* medicine!"

Gany folded his arms. "Uh huh. What are you supposed to be doing for your restitution?" Apollo looked away, mouth set mulishly. "Apollo? Where do you work?"

"I'm an orderly," he muttered, "at an assisted living facility. I have to wear rubber-soled shoes. And a *name tag*."

"So?"

"It's not even *my name*."

Despite himself, a smile tugged at Gany's lips. "What does it say?"

"Bob," Apollo spat. "Me! Do I look like a Bob to you? Everyone should know who I am. I had *altars. Priestesses.* Oracles! This is insupportable!"

"Did you ever think that your victims found *your* behavior insupportable?"

Apollo looked at Gany, his brow furrowed. "What?"

"Your victims. The people you hurt."

"I never hurt anybody!"

"Oh really? What about Marsyas? He was flayed alive for *losing* a music contest with you."

"That wasn't my fault. He shouldn't have challenged me."

"You nailed his skin to a *tree!*" When Apollo just shrugged, Gany said, "What about Daphne?"

"What about her? She's *immortal.*"

"She's a *tree*. Seriously, what is it with you and trees?"

"Her leaves are *iconic.*"

"I doubt that comforts her much, especially when there are bulldozers and climate change, and assholes with pocket knives who can destroy her at any time." Gany jabbed a finger toward Apollo's ridiculously broad chest. "The point of the Fates' decree is for you guys to *learn*. To *atone*. To become better people."

"We're not people," he said snootily. "We're gods."

"From where I'm standing? You're an orderly masquerading as an EMT who needs to stay far away from me if you don't want to spend eternity getting your liver excavated by an eagle."

Gany turned away, but as he was stalking back toward the ambulance, Apollo called, "Come on, Ganymede. I'll share the points with you."

"I don't need points," Gany replied. But as the fire truck drove away, Gany spotted the yellow police tape across Nectar & Ambrosia's storefront. *I need a new oven.*

"You can't want Zeus to get all the credit."

Gany skidded to a stop and turned slowly. "What do you mean?"

"If you come with me now," Apollo said, sidling toward Gany, "we can split the points four ways—you, me, Artemis, Hephaestus. We'll all get to Olympus faster than Zeus."

Gany rushed back and slapped his hand over Apollo's mouth. "Will you stop? For one thing, announcing that kind of thing in the middle of a Portland street is... well, I'm not sure exactly what it would mean, but I know it wouldn't be good. For another thing, I'm not going back."

Apollo batted Gany's hand away, looking sincerely confused. "Of course you are."

"No, I'm not. I don't know why you'd think so, but I don't have time to argue now. I have to go deal with the oven you assholes destroyed."

"It was for your own good. You might as well come with me now and avoid the hassle."

"The *hassle,* as you put it, wouldn't exist if you and your little gang had kept your Olympian noses out of my business. Goodbye, *Bob.* Don't come back."

"Ganymede—"

"I mean it." This time, he shoved his finger at Apollo's nose, practically up his left nostril. "You come near me again and I'm telling *all three* of the Fates."

Gany pivoted and stormed back toward the ambulance. He frowned when he spotted Courtland slamming its rear doors. Where was Finn? Was he inside? Were they taking him to the hospital?

"Ms. Courtland? Is Finn—"

"Oh, hey, Gary. Your friend is fine." She pointed down the alley. "I think he headed down there. Something about moving a car before it got towed?"

"Ah. Yes. Thank you."

"You sure you're okay?"

"Perfect. I promise."

That had always been his problem, hadn't it? Perfect beauty, enough to capture Zeus's wandering eye. And after millennia snacking on nothing but literal nectar and ambrosia, he'd never have a scar, never get sick. Even cuts from his chef's knives healed in a dozen heartbeats.

"If you're sure?"

"Yes, I…" Gany waved at her absently, craning his neck to see above the crowd still milling around the sidewalk. Was that…?

"Son of a harpy," he muttered, and took off at a run, dodging around the police cruiser and through a knot of onlookers to duck into the alley and confront Eros, who was huddling behind a dumpster.

"What are you doing here? I told you not to come back."

"I know, but—" His face scrunched and he stood, backing away from the dumpster. "What is that vile stench?"

"Rubbish. Trash. Refuse. It happens. You lot should know. You left a trail of it in your wake, only in your case, it wasn't rotting food, it was people and their ruined lives." He jerked his thumb toward where Apollo was still lurking at the edge of the crowd. "Are you part of this? Did you conspire with them to destroy my bakery?"

"What? No! I would never."

Gany crossed his arms. "Uh huh."

"I mean it. When have I ever destroyed anything?"

"You really want me to answer that?" Gany carded his hands through his hair and heaved a sigh. "Why are so many of you buzzing around me today? What's going on?

Apollo was going on about points. This is something with that stupid app, isn't it?" Eros's gaze slid away. "Ha! You do know! Spill."

Eros's eyes narrowed, his chest puffing out, and for an instant, Gany thought he'd hedge, but then his shoulders sagged. "You're a bonus quest."

Gany blinked. "I'm a what?"

Eros brandished his phone, the app glowing on its screen. "See, there are these side quests you can go on for extra points." He edged closer so Gany could see the list, which included things like *Feed the hungry, Be kind to animals, Help little old lady cross the street.*

"Seriously? You're gods on parole, not freaking Boy Scouts. And what do any of those have to do with me?"

"That's the perpetual list. You can do them over and over. They don't expire, but they're not worth many points." He swiped to that group graphic. One of the little icons was nearly at the top. "Hestia's hit that *feed the hungry* quest seven hundred and eighty-four times, and it's hardly fair. She works in a soup kitchen." Eros's tone was aggrieved. "Every time she dishes up a bowl of mac and cheese she gets points. She's going to get back to Olympus before the rest of us are halfway up the slope."

"Did you ever think she might not have as far to go?" Gany said dryly. "Her track record isn't as awful as the rest of you."

"Hmmmph." Eros tapped his screen to bring up another list. "These are the bonus quests. Onetime tasks. They've got way more points." He held it out. "See?"

Gany peered at the screen. At the top of a very short list —was his name—*Ganymede.* Just his name, no other details or description.

"See? If one of us brings you with us, we'll be right at the gates of Olympus in one step."

Gany stomach tumbled. *No.* The Fates wouldn't do this to him, would they? They'd promised him a life free of the gods. "How do you know?"

"How do I know what?"

"That you're supposed to bring me to Olympus?"

Eros blinked. "What else could it mean?"

"Since I never wanted to be in Olympus in the first place, maybe it means you *leave me alone!*"

Eros's perfect brow wrinkled. "You mean I'd get points for doing nothing?"

"No, you'd get points for letting me control my own life." Gany spotted Finn walking down the sidewalk toward them. "Now, if you'll excuse me, I need to figure out how to resurrect my business."

He left Eros frowning next to the dumpster and hurried to meet Finn, who was peering past Gany's shoulder, eyes narrowed.

"Isn't that the buff guy from the bakery this morning? Aaron?"

"Yes, but never mind him." Gany laid his palm against Finn's cheek, the stubble there surprisingly soft against his palm. "Are you okay?"

Finn placed his own hand over Gany's, holding it for an instant before he turned his head and kissed Gany's palm. "Never better. They gave me a hit off their oxygen and I'm good as new."

"You promise?"

"I do." He looked at the bakery. "You've got hazard insurance, right?"

"Of course."

"It'll probably take a while for them to pay out, though, won't it? How long do you think it'll take before you can replace the oven?"

Gany sighed and leaned against Finn's chest. "I've got the capital to replace it without waiting for the claim to go through, but you can't just pick up a commercial oven at the corner hardware store. It took three months for that last one to get delivered." He studied his cheerful pink-and-white striped awning. It hadn't been marred by the smoke, which was... something, anyway. "I can manage financially until the bakery reopens, but the catering business?" He looked up at Finn. "The wedding cake? I'll have to back out of the job."

Finn kissed him softly. "There'll be others. We'll just have to—"

"Gary Mead?"

Finn sucked in a sharp breath, his arms tensing around Gany. "M-M-Mr. Johnson?"

Gany looked around to find an extremely tall, extremely fit dark-haired man standing behind him, a smile on his genial, red-bearded face. The man—Mr. Johnson, apparently—nodded at Finn.

"Finn. Good to see you're back on your feet."

"I, um, thanks," Finn croaked.

Gany looked at him sharply. Did he need another hit of the EMT's oxygen? Were the EMTs gone? He craned his neck to look over Finn's shoulder, but Mr. Johnson cleared his throat, recapturing Gany's attention.

"Mr. Mead, I'm Rusty Johnson, of Johnson Construction. My crew and I are here to install your new oven."

Gany's jaw sagged. "My what?"

Mr. Johnson's eyebrows drew together. "Oven?" He nodded at a flatbed truck easing into the curb in front of the bakery.

"How did you know I needed one? *I* didn't even know until an hour ago."

"Really?" Mr. Johnson rubbed the back of his neck. "Del put in the order three months ago. The unit's been sitting in my warehouse for a week." He exchanged a cryptic look with Finn and chuckled awkwardly. "To be honest, I was afraid it wouldn't get here in time for the installation today. I had to call the vendor last week and goose them a bit. Do we have your okay to proceed?"

"I... Yes. Yes, of course. Do you..." Gany swallowed, hope kindling in his chest. "I don't suppose you have a timeline for me?"

"We'll be out of your hair in four hours or so. That'll give us time to repair any ancillary damage and get things cleaned up a bit."

"Th-thank you." He cuddled closer to Finn. "I'll be able to call for the inspections today, then. They always take some time to schedule, but—"

"Don't worry about that. Del scheduled those too. You'll be good to go by five o'clock, no problem." He saluted with three fingers and strode over to his crew, his flannel shirt flaring around his narrow hips.

"How?" Gany breathed. "How is this happening? Is it even possible?"

Finn was staring after Mr. Johnson, an extremely odd expression on his face. "If Rusty Johnson says he can do it, you can take that to the bank."

"You know him?"

"Yep. He's the best GC in the state. So if I were you, babe, I wouldn't worry about your oven anymore. Why don't we head home? You can whip up your cake samples in the kitchen there, and once Mr. Johnson gives you the go-ahead, you, Peyton, and Melina can head into the bakery and crush it."

"You really think so?"

"I more than think so. I *know* so." He kissed Gany's forehead. "Now I've got a Prius full of baking supplies with your name on 'em, so what do you say we get moving?"

Gany gave him a somewhat watery smile, but then straightened his shoulders and lifted his chin. "Works for me."

*Screw* the meddling gods. *With Finn beside me, I am absolutely going to crush it.*

# Chapter Eleven

"I know he said I'd be good to go, Finn, but I never thought I'd be *this* good!"

Finn tucked his phone close to his ear, as though that would bring Gary and his adorable enthusiasm closer, and tossed the Frisbee for the dogs for about the four hundred and eighty-seventh time. They took off after it like it was their first shot off the mark, even though they'd been playing non-stop for hours. It was nearly three in the morning, but the dogs were no more concerned by the darkness than Finn—and showed no sign of tiring of the game. Luckily, they were eerily quiet when they played, so Finn hadn't gotten any irate shouts from the neighbors.

He shook his arm out, flexing his fingers to ease their cramps, as the dogs played three-way tug-of-war with the Frisbee. Good thing he'd picked up half a dozen while he'd been on his bakery supply run.

"Like I said, if Mr. Johnson says something'll happen, it'll definitely happen."

"I mean, the place is *spotless*. Literally. I mean no spots of anything *anywhere*, including the freaking *ceiling*. The appliances are sparkling, the cabinets positively *glow*. They even cleaned out the walk-in fridge, which was completely unnecessary—its doors are massive, so no way could smoke have gotten inside. Mr. Johnson's crew must be magicians."

"Mmmphmm," Finn said. *Not magicians.* Finn had a strong suspicion that Rusty Johnson had brought along a brownie crew to handle cleanup. Nothing got past them. They took intense pride in the perfection of their work.

"Finn." Gary's voice dropped to a whisper, barely audible over Finn's lousy phone speaker. "They even replaced everything in the pantry. I barely even need the extra supplies you bought earlier. I mean, they replaced things that *weren't even there.*"

And *that* was another thing Finn couldn't comment on. Because Rusty had said *Del.* Del, who had ordered the new oven months ago. Del, who had arranged to send Rusty to the rescue the moment the firefighters departed. Del, who had scheduled inspections at *exactly the right time.*

In other words, Del, Hunter's Moon's manager.

The oracle.

The hope welling in Finn's chest made him want to bounce around like the pups. What did it mean that Del and Rusty were so involved in Gary's business? Could Gary be a supe? After all, Peyton *was* a witch, so maybe...

Gary didn't *smell* like any supe Finn had met before. Granted, most of his experience had been with other weres, and with the medimagical staff of St. Stupid's, which included not only werewolves but also witches, demons, an eight-tailed kitsune, and a team of achubyddion, the reclusive Welsh healers who'd emerged from hiding specifically to treat Hrodgar's Syndrome.

Finn had assumed Gary was just a really... fragrant human. Sweet and savory, wrapped together.

"Say, Gary?"

"Hmmm?"

"I never asked you. Whose wedding is this, anyway?"

"Oh. Heh. I never said, did I? I've only spoken to Del, who's one of the nearlyweds. Although, come to think of it, I never got a last name for them. Their fiancée is… Crap, I've got it written down somewhere." There was a low murmur and the sound of paper rustling. "Oh. Thanks, Peyton! Her name's Annemiek—wow, what a cool name! Annemiek Bakker."

Finn held his phone away and stared at it for a moment before gingerly pressing it to his ear. "*The* Annemiek Bakker?"

"You know who she is?"

"She's one of the most famous ballerinas in the world." And also a swan shifter. Fuck, this was a *supe* wedding. Del was probably involved because this was their own wedding and they wanted it to go off without a hitch, not because Gary was a supe. Fuck, Gary had *told* him the referral had come from Peyton. Supes used human businesses all the time without revealing themselves, and Peyton would know better than anybody how gifted Gary was with baked goods. "Where's this taking place?"

"At a resort called Wildwood? I'm not exactly sure of its location. Do you know it?"

Finn gulped. He knew it, all right. His father had shot him within half a mile of the place. Wildwood was owned by a grizzly shifter and his incubus husband—his *very protective* incubus husband, and the grizzly had been an early victim of Hrodgar's Syndrome.

"Finn? Are you still there?"

"Yeah. Yeah, I'm still... Listen, I—" Finn's throat closed as though he were still suffering from smoke inhalation.

Wildwood, where he'd have to face a whole ballroom full of supes, was the last place Finn wanted to be. The looks on their faces, the revulsion, the accusation, and when it came to the incubus, the fury. He couldn't face it. He couldn't—

"Finn? Is something wrong?"

The concern in Gary's voice nearly did him in. Concern for *Finn*, not for the cake or the job. The job Finn had *promised* to help with.

Fuck, he couldn't bail now. No way could Finn betray him by walking away when Gary needed him most.

Finn knew way too much about that kind of betrayal.

"No," he croaked, then cleared his throat and tried again. "Not a thing. When will you be home?"

"I've got everything frosted. Once I've added everything except the final decorations, I'll be home."

"I'll be waiting."

There was a silence on the other end of the phone. Finn winced. Did that sound too creepy? Maybe he should—

"I'm glad," Gary said softly. "I'll see you in a bit."

Finn sighed, hands trembling as he disconnected the call. Somehow, he'd have to pull up his big boy briefs tomorrow and face the wreckage of his past.

He stared down at the phone in his hand. *Maybe I need to face the hardest part first.*

Was it cowardly to leave the message on a voicemail? Maybe he should text. Somehow, this kind of apology over text seemed... low. A face-to-face meeting would be best, but voice-to-voice was the next best option. Well, voice-to-voicemail.

Finn took a deep breath and dialed Tanner's number, ready to grovel after the beep.

"Finn?"

Finn almost dropped the phone. "T-Tanner? Shit, sorry man. It's like the middle of the night. I didn't mean to wake you. I thought I could just leave a message and you could decide when or if you wanted to get back to me."

Tanner chuckled. "It's okay. I've been awake for a while. I'm in Savannah right now and I need to leave for the airport in about twenty minutes. What can I do for you?"

"Do for me? Remus's balls, Tanner, you shouldn't have to do anything for me, not after the way I treated you for almost our whole lives."

"Finn—"

"I'm so sorry for that. I can't excuse my behavior, and I wouldn't blame you if you never forgave me—"

"Finn—"

"—but I want you to know that I'm ready to do whatever you say, whatever you ask of me, to try to make amends. If you want me to leave, go far away, never speak to you—"

"Finn!"

Finn sucked in a breath, his instinct to sink down and bare his throat almost overwhelming, even though Tanner's alpha authority was dimmed by Finn's lousy cell phone speaker. *Gods, he must be lethal in person.*

"Yeah?"

"We're even."

"What? We can't be."

"Finn." Tanner's tone was patient, even kind. "You saved my life. You took two bullets for me."

"Yeah, but I didn't *know* that would happen!"

"You suspected *something* would happen. You knew Patrick better than I did, although it's clear neither one of us really knew him at all."

Finn swallowed thickly. "I was always trying to be good enough for him, you know? And since I never seemed to measure up, and I couldn't exactly take my frustrations out on *him*, I visited all my resentment on you. I'm really sorry about that. You didn't deserve any of that shit, especially since you weren't trying to curry his favor, anyway. He was just…"

"Grooming me?" Tanner said. "Lulling me? Fattening me up for eventual slaughter?"

"Yeah. That. All of that."

Tanner sighed. "Look, revenge has never really been my thing. I'm ready to call us more than square, especially if you're ready to move on and not victimize anyone anymore. I can't answer for anybody else, but you and me? We're good. Okay?"

The band that had constricted his chest since he'd realized what an asshole his father was finally eased. "Yeah. Okay. I'd like to catch up with you sometime. Find out how you're doing. *What* you're doing. All that shit."

"I'd like that," Tanner said softly. "I'll give you a call once I'm back in Portland and we'll set something up. Sound cool?"

"Absolutely. And Tanner?"

"Yeah?"

"Thanks."

Another chuckle. "Don't mention it, Finn. After all, we're pack. We've always been pack. Nothing will change that."

The call ended, and Finn looked down at the pups, who were gazing up at him, tails wagging, tongues lolling. Ozzie nudged the pitiful remains of a Frisbee toward Finn's feet.

"If we're gonna keep playing this game, guys, I'm gonna need to get somebody to bespell a few Frisbees, so you don't destroy them so fast." He patted each of their heads. "I doubt whether a protective enchantment from any spell-caster—witch, druid, or elemental mage—could stand up to your teeth, but maybe at least they could delay the inevitable."

"Finn?"

*Gary.* Had he heard Finn talking about spells? About druids and witches and mages? Fuck, did Gary *know* that Peyton was a witch? Finn's nose had tagged them for a supe that first day, but in all the time Finn had been haunting Nectar & Ambrosia, Peyton had maintained a totally human demeanor. It was possible Gary *didn't* know, and Finn wasn't about to out them.

"Um, over here. With the dogs."

When Gary emerged from around a massive rhododendron, he was smiling wide and bright, but even in the pale moonlight, Finn's werewolf sight could detect the dark circles under his eyes and the pinch between his brows, as though he hadn't yet noticed a headache.

He walked right into Finn's arms. *Where he belongs.* Finn kissed the top of his head and nuzzled the messy curls.

"Things go all right, then?"

Gary looked up at him, beaming. "*So* right. I literally couldn't believe what Mr. Johnson and his crew accomplished." His brows pinched tighter, deepening the furrow between them. "Although I still don't know how he could have been on the spot at precisely the right time." He chuckled. "It's almost like he could see the future."

Finn laughed weakly. "Yeah. Funny." He tilted Gary's chin up and kissed him. "But you're exhausted, sweetheart. Come to bed."

Gary's eyes widened. "I—"

"Hey. We talked about this. I'm not going to do anything you're not ready for. I just want to kiss you a little more and then hold you while you sleep."

Gary's brow cleared. "That sounds *divine*."

"What time do you need to be back at the bakery?"

"Probably about seven? I'm keeping it closed until Monday. We have all the supplies we need, but all the existing stock was lost. I've got a lot of prep to do."

"So…" Finn kept his tone deliberately casual. *Don't push, don't push.* "Does that mean Peyton and Melina will be able to help you serve the cake?"

"Hey." Gary captured Finn's face between his palms. "*You* are not off the hook, mister. I still need you. I'm *depending* on you."

Finn smoothed a curl off Gary's forehead. "You've got me. For as long as you need." *Forever.* "Now you need to get some rest."

With dogs bounding ahead of them, they headed for the house, Finn's arm around Gary's waist. Once inside, Finn paused long enough to give the pups an alpha glare and point them toward the three oversized dog beds in the corner of the living room. They only whined a little bit before each of them licked the back of his hand and slunk over to settle down, heads on their paws, but eyes still bright.

"Wow," Gary said. "You've really got a way with them."

Finn shrugged. "Like I said. I've got experience with canines. Now come on."

Gary was so bone-tired that he stood, soft and compliant, while Finn gently undressed him down to his pink designer briefs. "Do you want to take another shower?" They'd both showered after they'd gotten home after the fire, just to purge the stench of smoke off of themselves.

He wrinkled his nose. "I probably should. I must stink."

Finn nuzzled Gary's neck, and there it was again. That singular, incredible, seductive scent that had tickled his nose the first time he'd seen Gary behind the cash register.

"You smell just as delicious as you always do. But sometimes a shower can help you relax."

Gary laughed, leaning his forehead against Finn's chest. "I may not precisely be relaxed—too much riding on this gig tomorrow—but I don't think I've got the spoons to stand up another minute."

"Then come here." Finn lifted Gary and cradled him against his chest.

Gary sighed. "Why do I feel so safe in your arms?"

"Because you are." He settled Gary in the bed and pulled the blankets up over his shoulders. "I will never, *ever* let anything bad happen to you."

"I know," Gary murmured, his eyes already fluttering closed. "I've always known."

Inside Finn's chest, right below his heart, his calon blazed, afire with unprecedented certainty. *So have I.*

He shucked off his own clothes, but left his boxer briefs on, grateful he'd had a chance to do laundry while Gary was at the bakery. He didn't want Gary to feel the least pressure to give Finn any more than he was ready for.

He slotted himself behind Gary, spooning him, and dropped one last kiss on his nape before he closed his eyes.

But in what seemed like the next instant, he was wide awake, scrambling out of bed. He peered at the digital clock on the nightstand. Almost six.

All three dogs were going nuclear—barking and growling and, judging from the thumps emanating from the living room, throwing themselves against the door. The double-paned glass was tempered, but it wouldn't stand up to that kind of onslaught for long.

"What's happening?" Gary said sleepily.

"Something's got the dogs riled. You stay in bed. I'll get them settled."

He waited until Gary collapsed back on his pillow, then strode out of the bedroom and down the hall, unleashing his full alpha authority.

"Boys," he barked, "what the... *Holy fucking shit.*"

Beyond the dogs, who looked even bigger than usual with their hackles bolt upright, an enormous eagle— Remus's balls, that wingspan had to be twenty feet if it was an inch—hovered over the patio with barely a twitch of its wings.

Finn heard the shuffle of bare feet on the carpet behind him, along with Gary swearing in some other language.

"Stay back," Finn said, unlocking the door.

"No, Finn." Gary grabbed his arm. "You don't understand. It's—"

In a burst of white light and a clap of thunder, the eagle transformed into a man.

# Chapter Twelve

Gany was so furious he could have hurled one of Zeus's stupid lightning bolts straight at the big jerk's head. What was he *doing* here? He wasn't *allowed*. Gany lunged for the door. He was going to give Zeus a piece of his mind. He was going to—

"Gary, no." Finn gathered Gany to his chest and turned them both so Finn's back was to the door, effectively blocking Gany's view of Zeus. "Look, I don't know who this guy is, or what I did for the council to send him after me, but I promise I won't let him hurt you."

"Finn—"

"I talked to Tanner earlier, and he said everything was cool between us, but he couldn't answer for anyone else, so I guess somebody's decided to make a move."

"Finn—"

"I'll give myself up. It doesn't matter what they do to me. My life was trash before I met you anyway, so I *mmmphm*."

Gany shut him up by kissing him. When he drew back, Finn was blinking as though he'd been smacked in the head with a cast-iron skillet.

"Uh..." Finn said.

"Are you ready to listen now?" When Finn nodded warily, Gany pointed over his shoulder. "He's not here for you, honey."

"How do you know?" An odd, hopeful light dawned in Finn's eyes. "You know about shifters?"

Gany huffed a laugh. "He's not a shifter. Well, I mean he does transform himself into other things—a swan, a bull, a shower of gold, an *eagle*." Gany stopped ranting long enough to glare over Finn's shoulder at Zeus, because this was how Gany had first seen him, right before Zeus had plucked him off the hillside and carried him off to Olympus. "But he's not a shapeshifter, per se."

"Ganymede," Zeus bellowed.

Gany winced. Between Zeus using his outdoor voice and the dogs objecting vociferously to Zeus's presence, the neighbors were *not* going to be happy about the racket.

Finn angled himself slightly so he could look outside, but still blocked Gany's body with his own. It was... sweet, but unnecessary.

"If he's not a shifter, then..." He glanced down at Gany, eyebrows quirked.

Gany sighed, because Zeus's zest for drama made it impossible to pass him off as anything other than what he was. "He's Zeus, Finn, and I need to talk to him before he literally wakes the dead."

Finn's eyes popped wide. "Zeus. You mean *the* Zeus? Like from Greek mythology?"

Gany smiled a little crookedly. "To you, it's mythology. To us, it's just our big, dysfunctional family history." He gestured to the door. "Could you keep the dogs contained? I really have to..."

Finn moved out of the way, although he stuck close enough that Gany could feel the warmth of his bare chest against Gany's back. Gany opened the door and stepped outside. Behind him, Finn murmured something to the dogs before sliding the door closed. The dogs' growls were only slightly muffled by the glass, but at least they weren't barking.

With Finn's hand warm on the small of his back, Gany crossed his arms and glared up at Zeus, who was wearing a minuscule speedo, his broad, bare, muscled chest glistening in the fading moonlight. *Probably oiled it up just for the occasion.* Zeus was even more vain than Narcissus.

"You're not supposed to be here, Zeus. According to the terms of your parole, you can't step over the threshold."

"I didn't *step* over the threshold." With a smirk, Zeus spread his arms wide and waggled his fingers. "I flew."

"The result is the same. You're here where you shouldn't be. You're not allowed to approach any of your victims."

Zeus's alabaster brow wrinkled. "But I'm here to *fix* that, Ganymede. To apologize. To make amends."

Gany's eyebrows shot up of their own accord. Zeus apologizing? He *never* apologized for anything. And how in hades did he expect to make amends for kidnapping? For sexual assault? For enslavement?

Gany lowered his brows and narrowed his eyes. "Let's hear it, then."

Zeus folded his hands in front of himself. He probably thought it made him look nonthreatening and repentant, but considering he was framing his dick between his wrists, it wasn't really hitting the right note.

On the other hand, this was *Zeus*. The dick shot was probably intentional.

"I was remiss in my care of you. I should have engaged more fully. Protested when Tyche ordered you to toil in the Purgatory kitchens."

"It wasn't an order. I volunteered. And it was the best kind of toil. I had a blast."

"A blast?" Zeus's chest expanded and his eyes blazed. "Did Hephaestus steal one of my lightning bolts again? He thinks just because he makes the ammo that he's entitled to raid the inventory."

Gany rolled his eyes. "Not that kind of blast."

Zeus lifted one hand in the royal wave. "In any case, as it's not relevant to this moment, I shall let the transgression pass. Let's talk about us." He gazed down at Gany with what he probably thought was an earnest expression. "I'm here to mend things with you, Ganymede. To take you home."

Gany frowned. "I am home."

Zeus *tsk*ed. "You needn't suffer in this hovel, not when Olympus awaits." He lowered his voice and leered. "Awaits us both."

"So let me get this straight." Gany dropped his hands to his sides, fists clenched. "You're not apologizing for taking me to Olympus in the first place, but for letting me leave?"

Bewilderment flickered across Zeus's broad face. "Of course."

"I don't freaking believe it," Gany muttered.

"I tried to tell him!"

Gany whirled to see Eros peering over the fence from the neighbor's yard. "Oh, for fuck's sake," he muttered, grateful to Finn for teaching him that particular phrase. It was so *useful*, not to mention expressive.

"Stay out of this, Eros," Zeus hollered. "This isn't your affair."

"No, it's not," Gany said. "It's not yours either, Zeus, but it's most definitely mine. I never wanted to go to Olympus in the first place, I didn't want to *stay* there, and now that I've escaped, I'm never going back."

"You don't mean that, Ganymede," Zeus said with an indulgent smile. "If you did, the app wouldn't say so."

"Are you going to listen to an app or me? I'm telling you, no."

Zeus chuckled. "That's what they all say at first."

"Then you should *listen*. You're not entitled to everything—to every*body*—you want just because you're the guy with the biggest throne."

"Nonsense. Once we're home—"

"He told you no." Finn's voice, backed by the slide of the door, was nearly as growly as the dogs'.

Uh oh.

Gany glanced over his shoulder. And blinked.

Finn was naked.

But before he could blink a second time, Finn was…

A wolf. A really *big* wolf, black and shaggy, with two moon-white spots on his shoulder.

*All righty, then.*

Finn-the-wolf approached Zeus, ears flattened and teeth bared, as Sir, Bear, and Ozzie, eyes glowing, growls vibrating in their throats, circled until Zeus was surrounded by four really pissed off canines.

"*I've got experience with canines,*" Finn had said. Gany would have laughed if he wasn't terrified of what Zeus would do to them all.

But surprisingly, Zeus drew himself in like a Victorian matron cowering on a chair from a mouse.

"Call them off," he said, voice an octave higher than its usual thunderous bass.

Gany slapped his forehead. *Of course.* None of the gods could get past Cerberus, not even Hades.

"You know," Gany said, rocking back on his heels. "I don't think I can. I'm pretty sure they answer to him now." He placed his hand on Finn's back, the fur surprisingly soft and plush under his fingers. "And just between us? I don't think he's in a forgiving mood, so you need to leave. Now. Before I let the Fates know you tried to game the system."

"But the quest! Your name is *right there.* How will I get back to Olympus without those points?"

"Not my problem," Gany said, with zero remorse. "Now get out of here. Go on." He flapped his hands. "Fly away."

For an instant, Gany thought Zeus would make a grab for him anyway, but then Finn growled, and, along with the three dogs, crept closer, Finn's eyes trained on Zeus's midsection as his jaws parted and he lowered into a crouch, ready to spring.

And that did it. Zeus took eagle form and launched himself skyward, Finn tracking his flight with a laser-focused gaze.

Once Zeus disappeared into the gray, pre-dawn sky, Finn shifted back, and he was naked again.

"Oooh la la," Eros crooned.

Finn, however, seemed unconcerned. He just scooped his boxer briefs off the patio and pulled them on.

"So," Gany said. "Werewolf?"

"So," Finn replied with a quirk of his eyebrow. "Greek god?"

Gany scrunched his face. "Ugh. No. I'm human, same as—" He choked. "I was about to say same as you, but… well…" He shrugged.

"Human?" Eros scoffed from his spot at the fence. "Riiight."

Gany glared at him. "Shut up, Eros. I'm a shepherd's kid from Dardania who had the bad luck to catch Zeus's eye."

"So you started out human. So what?" Eros winked at Finn. "You tell me, handsome. How many humans do *you* know that are several thousand years old and still look that good?"

Gany bit his lip, gazing up at Finn, whose cheeks were far too hollow and whose ribs far too visible under his pale skin. "Were you going to tell me?"

Finn sighed and carded his hands through his hair, which was *definitely* shaggier than it had been before. "We're not allowed. There's a whole"—he made a helpless gesture—"*thing* about keeping our community secret from humans." He fisted his hands on his hips, directly above his pronounced iliac furrow, and glared at Eros. "Do *you* know about the community?"

"You mean, did I know you were a werewolf? Did I know that Ganymede's therapist is fae? That one of his employees is a witch?"

"Wait," Gany spluttered. "What?"

Finn rolled his eyes. "Great. *Now* you've done it."

Eros grinned. "Exactly. *I've* done it. So no Secrecy Pact violations for you." He placed one hand on the fence and vaulted into the yard, even though the fence was eight feet tall. Gany suspected he did it just to show off—he could have levitated without all the drama. He smoothed down his shirt and pulled out his phone. "Carry on."

"Your name is really Ganymede?" Finn asked. "You're *that* Ganymede? The one from the myths?"

"Like I said. Not myths to us." Gany quirked an eyebrow. "Do *you* like to be called a fairy tale? Legend? Fiction?"

Finn's smile was wry. "We actually prefer it, the better to stay hidden. The consequences of exposure are… Well, let's say the danger isn't only from the human torch-and-pitchfork brigade."

"I'd like to know more about it. About you. But—"

"Ha!" Eros thrust one fist in the air, the other brandishing his phone. "Check it out. Zeus fell *all* the way to the bottom. We're all ahead of him now, even Hades."

"Congratulations," Gany said dryly.

"Wait," Finn said. "What's going on with these guys, anyway?"

Gany huffed an exasperated breath. "They're *supposed* to be atoning for their past behavior. Making restitution to their victims." Gany swiveled to face Eros and raised his voice. "Becoming better people."

Eros frowned. "Easy for you to say. I mean, look at Zeus. He thought he was making restitution to you, but he got bounced to the bottom of the hill for it. How are we supposed to know how to fix things?"

"You can do what I did," Finn said with a shrug. "Admit you were wrong. Apologize."

Eros looked sincerely bewildered. "What?"

"Tell whoever you hurt that you're sorry and *ask them* what you can do to make amends."

"But... but that's *humiliating!*"

"Trust me, I know. But"—Finn shrugged again—"you did the crime, pal. This is how you do the time."

The dogs' ears perked up, and all three heads swiveled to look at the open door an instant before Gany heard his phone ringing faintly from the bedroom.

Finn shook his head. "That's so weird. It's like they're one... Wait a minute." He goggled. "Sir. Bear. Ozzie. They're not— You— This isn't—"

Gany patted his arm. "Yes. They used to be Cerberus. They get a second chance too. But that's my phone, so..."

Gany rushed inside and down the hall to the bedroom to scoop up his phone from the nightstand. "Hello?"

"Hey, Gary. This is Del. Sorry for the late call, but it looks as though we'll need more than one server to help with your cake. They'll be compensated, of course."

With the bakery closed until Monday, Melina and Peyton would be free. "Would three be enough?"

"Six would be better. You'll manage it. The other caterers will be using the main Wildwood kitchen, but there's a secondary kitchen next to it. It's a bit smaller and is used for... specialty work."

"Specialty? You mean like pastry?"

"Something like that. You can set up there any time after eight." Del chuckled. "Now, I've got to run. It's my wedding day."

Gany stared at the phone after Del disconnected. Where was he going to get three more servers? He couldn't exactly rope Eros, Artemis, and Apollo into service. That would be begging for trouble.

"Hey." Finn was suddenly there, wrapping an arm around Gany's waist and kissing the spot between his eyebrows. "What's wrong?"

"I somehow have to find three more servers for the wedding, in addition to you and Peyton and Melina." He paused, one of Eros's comments coming back to him. "And what did he mean, one of my employees is a witch?"

Finn chuckled and kissed Gany's lips softly. "We'll talk. In the meantime, as for servers, I might know some guys." Finn kissed him again. "Don't worry, sweetheart. My pack has got your back."

# Chapter Thirteen

"Whoa." Hector—one of Tanner's Doghouse pack mates who'd volunteered to help when Finn called—stared into the Nectar & Ambrosia window, his nose nearly pressed against the glass. "I didn't know this place was here."

"It opened a few months ago," Finn said. "I've been coming every day since then. My, ah, boyfriend owns it." Finn buried a wince at the *B* word, not because he didn't *want* it or because *he* wasn't there yet, but because he and Gary—no, *Gany*, and Finn still couldn't wrap his head around *that* little piece of intel—hadn't put a name on what they were yet.

"Awesome." Gage, one of the other guys, patted his flat stomach. "Think they'll have any snacks for us today? Always room for pastries, am I right?"

"I'm not sure. There was an incident yesterday. Not quite a fire, but all the existing stock was ruined. Gan—Gary's keeping the place closed until Monday so he can focus on this wedding."

"Cool." Dakota, the third member of the trio, grinned at Finn. "We'll come over and help celebrate the reopening. But for now, let's get this done." He smoothed his hands down his white button-down and patted the seat of his black jeans. "Will we have monogrammed aprons? I've always wanted a monogrammed apron."

Hector lifted both eyebrows. "You have? Why?"

Dakota shrugged. "When people have their names actually stitched onto their clothes it feels, I dunno, special."

"Don't hold your breath," Finn said. "There might be aprons, but I doubt your names'll be on them. Gary doesn't even know what your names *are* yet."

He beckoned them to follow him down the alley to the back door. Hector trotted to keep up. Of the three guys, he was the only one who looked as though he hadn't fully recovered from Hrodgar's Syndrome yet, and the way his white shirt bagged on him and his black jeans sagged from a cinched-in belt threatened to swamp Finn with guilt again.

But they'd all cheerfully agreed to help, with no recriminations or demands for quid pro quo. In fact, when he'd tried to apologize to them, Gage had stared at him.

"Dude, for what? It's not like you can choose your parents. Besides, you *literally* took a bullet for Tanner. We're cool."

So Finn decided to roll with it. He mounted the concrete ramp and rapped on the back door, the metal booming hollowly under his fist, then backed up a step, leaving room.

With a clang of the panic bar, Peyton opened the door and grinned at them. "Hey."

Finn heard a gasp behind him and turned to see Dakota gaping, wide-eyed, at Peyton. *Well, isn't that interesting?* Finn hid his smile.

"Hey, Peyton. This is Hector, Gage, and Dakota, my—"

"His pack." Dakota shouldered his way past Hector and Gage to hold out his hand. "Love the eyeliner."

Peyton cut a rather alarmed glance at Finn as they shook Dakota's hand. "Th-thanks."

"Do you need a familiar?"

Another wide-eyed glance at Finn. "Um. Sorry. What? Familiar?"

Finn tapped his nose. "We're all weres," he murmured, checking that Melina was out of earshot. "We can tell you're a witch."

"Oh." Peyton lost a bit of their deer-in-the-headlights expression, but kept their voice low. "Then yes, I have a familiar."

"Cool!" Dakota grinned. "What kind?"

"Sugar glider."

"Really? Those little squirrellish dudes who can fly? Aren't they from Australia or someplace?"

Peyton smiled shyly. "Not fly. Just glide. And yes, Australia. She was exhausted when she finally reached me at my Partnering Ceremony, even though the triple goddess helped her on the journey." Peyton pushed the door wider. "Come on in. I made scones."

That seemed to light a fire under the Doghouse guys, and they trooped inside, Finn gesturing for Peyton to precede him before he closed the door.

This was the first time Finn had been in the kitchen when it hadn't been obscured by smoke. Now he was met by bright, warm lighting, countertops in marble, wood, and steel, and gleaming commercial appliances.

One of the steel prep tables held three round cake layers in graduating sizes, the biggest about a foot and a half across, all of them frosted in smooth, white icing. Gany was standing on a step-stool in front of five assembled tiers, pastry bag in hand as he studied the curve of the swan's neck above the top tier.

The swan was exquisite, exactly as Gany had sketched it, so lifelike that Finn could swear if he touched a feather, it would be soft.

It was also *way* more appropriate than Gany knew.

"Wow," Hector breathed.

"I know, right?" Finn whispered, not wanting to distract Gany at this delicate stage.

"What are those things?" Hector pointed to a ring of what looked like glass or clear acrylic dowels, about an inch across, embedded in each of the unassembled tiers.

"Support rods for the separator plates," Peyton said as they skirted the table, a platter of scones in their hands. "Stabilizes the structure. Cake doesn't sit directly on top of cake or it would all compress and collapse." They held out the platter. "Here you go, guys. Grab a snack before we go."

"Go?" Gany fumbled the pastry bag, but Finn darted forward to catch it before it could fall. "Dam*nation*, I *forgot*."

"Forgot what, sweetheart?"

Gany turned stricken eyes up to Finn. "I forgot to buy a *van*. I was going to do it when I got my first catering gig, but I expected more lead time, and then with the oven and the"—he cut a glance at Peyton and Melina—"*visitations*, I forgot. How are we going to get this cake to the venue? I can't load it into TD's Prius. How am I supposed to get it to Wildwood?"

Finn eyed the assembled tiers, embraced by the delicate swan. "You know, babe, even if you had a van, I don't think the cake could have made the trip intact. Wildwood is like an hour and a half away, and some of those roads are pretty winding."

"Oh, no!" Gany practically tumbled off the stool and into Finn's arms. "I should have waited to assemble it at the venue. I didn't think... I've never made anything this big before, and..." He paled. "Did you say an hour and a half?"

"About that, yeah."

He clutched Finn's shirt. "What time is it?"

"Quarter to eight," Hector said around a mouthful of scone.

"Oh, hades," Gany moaned. "Even if I can find a van and the cake doesn't disintegrate on the road, I'd never make it in time. The wedding is at ten." Gany dropped his forehead against Finn's chest. "How can I expect to run a catering business, a *wedding cake* business, if I make this kind of mistake? Before I never had to worry about delivery. I mean, on Olympus, the gods were just always *there*, and they never wanted anything but stupid nectar and ambrosia anyway."

Finn darted a glance at Peyton, whose jaw was sagging, and then at Melina, whose expression read sympathetic understanding rather than shock. "Um..."

Melina held up a hand and waggled her fingers. "Hi, folks. I'm Melina. Barista, baker's assistant, aaannnd former Vestal."

"Vestal?" Hector wiped his hands on his jeans, leaving scone crumbs behind. "Like Vestal Virgin?"

Melina scrunched up her nose. "Yeah, one little problem with that. Couldn't serve the goddess without that virginity requirement, and when another god deprives you of that—right in front of the altar, I might add—guess who gets the blame." She shook her head. "I suppose I shouldn't complain. At least I didn't get turned into a gorgon like poor Medusa. Hestia/Vesta is a lot more laidback than Athena."

"So..." Finn leaned back so he could look down into Gany's face. "In that case, I'm guessing all secrets are out? If Melina is like you, then you've probably figured out that Peyton is the witch."

Gany grimaced. "Yes, but we haven't had *time* to get into that, and anyway, I don't care. *This* disaster"—he flung a hand out at the cake—"is the problem now. I'll have to call Del and tell them I can't fulfill the contract."

"Not so fast." Finn exchanged a glance with the Doghouse guys, who all shrugged. "There's another way. But it's... complicated."

Peyton's eyes widened. "You don't mean—"

"Yep. We're taking a shortcut." Finn held Peyton's gaze. "Can you manage a levitation spell?"

Peyton's brows drew together, eyes losing focus as they thought. "Yes. But I'll need some ingredients from my apartment." They glanced apologetically at Gany. "And I'll need my familiar. I know bringing an animal into the bakery is—"

"Can you set a no-shed spell on her?" Finn asked.

Peyton brightened. "Yeah. Yes, I can do that." They untied their bib apron and lifted it over their head to hang it on a hook under a shelf holding nests of brightly colored ceramic bowls. "I won't be ten minutes." They rushed out the door, letting it *clang* shut behind them.

Finn kissed Gany's forehead and turned him gently within the circle of his arms so he faced the Doghouse guys. "Gany—or would you prefer to stick with Gary?"

"Either one is fine, just *please* don't call me Ganymede!"

Finn chuckled. "No problem. Gany, meet Gage, Hector, and Dakota. From my… my pack."

"Hi," Gany said faintly. "Thanks so much for being willing to help out."

"No worries there," Dakota replied. "If you're with Finn, you're pack too. And besides"—he brandished a scone—"you can always capture a were's heart with food like this."

Finn gnawed his lower lip and moved aside so they were standing in a loose circle, although he kept his fingers laced with Gany's. "Here's the thing. We need to call an FTA driver, but I'm broke, and I don't have a ride token."

"That's not a problem." Hector dug his phone out of his pocket. "I've got an app for that."

Finn lifted an eyebrow. "An app? When did the supe community embrace modern human tech? I haven't been out of touch *that* long."

Hector shifted from foot to foot. "It's, um, not entirely sanctioned. Does that bother you?"

"Me?" Finn snorted. "I'd go a lot farther than one sketchy app call to save Gany's cake gig. Go for it."

Hector glanced around the kitchen. "It's kind of cramped in here, but we can hardly go somewhere else to open the portal."

Gage pointed to the massive walk-in fridge door. "What about opening that? I mean, the drivers can appear out of nowhere, but they always like a door when one's available. Something about sympathetic transformational magic or whatever."

"How do you know that?"

Gage shrugged. "Had a chat with a couple of fae drivers a while back."

"We can hardly leave the fridge doors open behind us."

"Oh, that won't be a problem. Once the driver comes through, we can close 'em. They can open the portal *through* the doors on the way back."

"All right," Finn said, "then here's what—"

"Excuse me?" Gany raised his hand and waved it in the air above his head, like a grade school kid who knew the answer to the teacher's question. "I don't mean to be ungrateful, Finn, but what's going on? What's the FTA, and why do you imagine someone can drive through my walk-in fridge?"

"Oh." Finn blinked, suddenly realizing he might have bulldozed ahead without sharing a few pertinent details. "Sorry. The FTA is the Fae Transportation Association. The King and Queen of Faerie put it in place to give their people new employment opportunities since the traditional ones—stampeding cows, souring milk, kidnapping humans—are frowned upon these days. We— that is, any supe—can call an FTA driver and they'll escort us through Faerie." He smoothed the wrinkle between Gany's brows. "Don't worry. It won't be a long hike. Faerie's kind of like the closest distance between any two points. You can get from anywhere *to* anywhere with about a ten-minute walk, provided both endpoints are hidden from humans."

"Wait." Gany's eyes had gotten wider and wider during Finn's explanation. "You're saying we're going to *Faerie*? Like, that's a real place?"

Finn smirked at him. "Like, Olympus is a real place?"

Gany rolled his eyes. "Fine. Point taken, but—"

Peyton burst through the back door, panting, a bright-eyed, gray and black furred creature about the size of a hamster, with a tail longer than its body, clinging to their shoulder, a linen-wrapped bundle in their arms. "Got it." They jerked their head sideways at the little sugar glider. "This is Nerida, everyone. My familiar."

"Nice to meet you, um, Nerida." Gany huddled next to Finn. "Will this take long, Peyton?"

"No more than five minutes. I'm going to bespell that" —they pointed to a wheeled, multi-shelved metal cart that came up to Finn's waist—"so we can transport all the pieces at once. You and Melina can transfer the cakes onto it while I work."

"Should we wait to call the driver until after you're done?" Finn asked as Peyton began laying out the spell ingredients on a marble-topped counter farthest from the cakes, their familiar watching with intense focus.

"No. You can go ahead. This isn't too complicated."

"Got it."

Finn nodded to Hector, who approached the fridge with his cell phone in his hand. He touched the screen and a digital voice said, "*Cludo*."

"Where to?" said a deep, gravelly voice that emanated from inside the fridge. "Why's it so cold?"

"Hey, Frang," Hector said. "We need to get to Wildwood."

"Wildwood?" A hulking duergar in a sleeveless leather jerkin and homespun trousers ducked his head and stepped out of the fridge, briskly rubbing his enormous hands over his greenish pebbled skin. "I don't know. There's a wedding there today. Humans'll be around, so I can't get too close."

"Can you gate us right inside the resort?" Finn asked.

"The secondary kitchen." Gany's voice was a little choked. Finn could hardly blame him if this was his first time facing a duergar. "We're cleared to work there."

"Is that possible?" Finn asked Frang.

"Why not?" Frang shrugged. "It's your gold."

Peyton, Nerida's rear claws clinging to their shoulder and front paws on their chest, held their hands out, palms forward. The cart, the five-tiered cake on the top and the single layers on the shelves underneath, the lowest shelf stocked with kitchen tools, bags, and boxes, lifted smoothly into the air and hovered about six inches above the floor. When Peyton paced slowly toward the fridge, the cart floated ahead of them without so much as a wobble.

Gany clasped his hands under his chin. "Oh!"

Finn gazed down at him fondly, noting that his knuckles were speckled with white frosting. "Pretty cool, huh? Although you're probably used to magic."

"Not like this. Oops, almost forgot." Gany hurried to a shelf next to the ovens and retrieved a stack of pink-and-white striped cloth. "I've got aprons for all of you."

"Monogrammed?" Dakota asked hopefully.

Gany bit his lip, lifting one shoulder. "Nope. Sorry."

"No worries," Dakota said. "Can't have everything, I guess. We'll just be your anonymous, but totally hot and efficient, staff." He saluted. "Onward!"

Frang stood next to the portal that overlaid the closed fridge door as Dakota, Gage, Melina, and then Hector followed Peyton through into a lush green Faerie meadow.

"Ready?" Finn asked Gany.

Gany lifted his rather pointed chin determinedly. "Absolutely." He shifted the aprons to one arm and captured Finn's hand, lacing their fingers together. "Let's go." But before they'd gone more than two steps, he stopped. "Just a minute." He darted back to the platter that had held Peyton's towering stack of scones, but now sported only three, thanks to the depredations of the Doghouse guys. Gany snatched the platter and offered it to Frang. "Would you like a scone?"

Frang blinked, peat-brown eyes going a little glassy. "For me?"

"If you want them."

"Nobody ever gave me *food* for a tip before." He took one scone almost daintily, given that his fingers were the size of kielbasa.

"I'll save some cake for you, too," Gany promised, "in case you come back to pick us up again."

This time, Frang's eyes positively glowed. "Cake?" He grabbed the remaining two scones and shooed them forward. "Let's go."

"I've got to say, walking through my closed fridge door isn't anything I thought I'd ever—" Gany's amused words cut off with a gasp. "Gods, it's *beautiful*." He scanned the landscape, from the burbling stream that bisected the meadow to the tree-topped tor that rose beyond it. "Is the sky actually *orange*?"

"Not all the time. It's a color spectrum—red in the morning, violet at night, and everything else in between."

"I don't think I've ever—"

"No dawdling," Frang said as he stomped past them. "Cake is waiting."

"Well, then," Finn said, "guess we better get moving."

Laughing, they hurried after him as he passed the other weres and then Peyton, although he slowed reverently as he tiptoed past the cake. He stopped next to a boulder about fifty yards away from where they'd entered.

"Frang?" Hector said hesitantly, "this isn't one of the approved FTA routes."

"Screw the approved routes," Frang growled. With a wave of one enormous hand, the boulder vanished as a portal opened into what was clearly a commercial kitchen. "There's cake!"

# Chapter Fourteen

Gany held his breath as the cart with the cake came to a gentle stop next to a long metal prep table and settled gently onto its wheels. Muffled conversation, clinks, and clatters filtered in from the main kitchen beyond a swinging door where the caterers must be preparing the wedding brunch. For a moment, a little spear of envy pierced Gany's relieved satisfaction, but he sternly brushed it aside as though it were one of Eros's unwanted arrows.

He couldn't pine about lost catering jobs when his first wedding cake was *here*, perfect and beautiful and waiting for final assembly.

Which… might not happen. He sighed. *Backup cake, remember?* But even if they didn't serve the cake to the wedding guests, at least his crew—Peyton, Melina, Finn, Finn's werewolf buddies, and apparently Frang, who hadn't left after he'd escorted them through the portal—could taste it later. And *somehow* Gany would make sure that Del at least had a chance to taste it too.

Peyton's arms flopped to their sides. "Whew! That was harder than I thought it would be. I feel like I just escaped from extreme arm day at the gym." They rubbed their cheek against Nerida's fur. "Thanks, love." They patted the front of their apron, where one big pocket was divided in two by a row of vertical stitching. "Into your pouch now."

Nerida nosed Peyton's cheek, then scampered down, clinging to the fabric with tiny claws. Peyton held the left pocket open and she dove in. "Oh, I almost forgot."

They reached into the right pocket and pulled out a handful of shiny objects. "It's not monogramming, I know, but I made name tags for you all that match the ones we use at Nectar & Ambrosia. Finn?" They held out the little gold rectangle and Finn took it almost reverently. The other weres gathered around Peyton to collect their own badges.

Dakota donned his apron and pinned the badge to the center of the bib, in exactly the right place. "I feel so official."

Finn, his own name tag in place, grinned at Gany. "I feel like I belong."

Gany smiled back. "You do. And, um..." He bit his lip and peered up at Finn through his lashes. "I hope that after we're done here, you'll still feel that way."

"I do. I mean, I will. That is, I'm sure, but..." Finn grimaced, squinting one eye. "There might be... issues. Werewolves aren't really allowed to form, um, romantic relationships with non-weres."

"Dude." Hector's voice was muffled because his chin was tipped all the way down as he tried to pin his name tag on. "That's old school stuff. I'm pretty sure Tanner's got that on his list of shit that needs to change."

"Really?"

Hector finally fastened the pin. He patted the badge and looked up at Finn with a half-smile. "You'd know if you'd spent any time with us."

"Yeah," Gage said, clapping Finn on the shoulder. "Stop being such a lone wolf."

Gany lifted both eyebrows when a visible shudder ran through all four werewolves at once. "I'm guessing that as a group, you're not fans of solitude?"

Dakota shrugged. "What can I say? We're pack animals." He winked. "Even when we're human."

Frang edged past them all to a tall stool in the corner, which creaked audibly when he sat on it. Gany peered at the bundle of tall *somethings*—black, white, and red—in a niche at Frang's elbow.

"Are those *candles*? Hades, they're practically as big around as my waist!"

Next to him, Finn chuckled. "Wildwood hosts supe events as well as human ones. I'm pretty sure this kitchen is for *alternative* kinds of cooking, if you get my drift."

"Yeah, Del said it was for specialty... Wait a minute." Gany's eyes widened. "You mean *magic*?"

"Don't sound so gobsmacked," Melina said, shifting supplies from the cart's lowest shelf to the prep table. "You concocted nectar and ambrosia for the Olympians for thousands of years."

"Yeah, but that wasn't magic. It was just"—Gany flapped his hands helplessly—"*Olympus*."

"Like I said, Gany." She smirked at him with the largest separator plate in one hand. "Magic."

"Oh. Well. Okay." Gany rubbed his hands on the front of his apron. "I guess. When you put it *that* way."

The door next to Frang swung open, and Gany caught a glimpse of the ballroom beyond, tables draped in pristine white linens and set with crystal, china, and silver.

"Good morning," said the person on the threshold, whose chin-length hair was dyed in a vibrant rainbow. "I'm Del. I'm happy you made it here safely." They nodded to Frang. "For which we have you to thank, Frang. You have my gratitude."

Del was clearly in their wedding outfit—not precisely a tux, but over an elaborately pleated V-neck white shirt, they were wearing a black coat, cropped at their narrow waist in the front, short tails extending to mid-thigh in the back. The sides of the jacket, as well as the outer seams of their slim-cut black trousers, sparkled with crystals that echoed their rainbow locks.

They approached the cake, a smile curving their rather austere mouth. "It's as stunning as I imagined. Just as perfect as I knew it would be." They turned to Gany and held out their hand. "Thank you so much."

Gany shook hands. "It was my pleasure. Even if we're not able to serve it—"

"Oh you will," Del said, their smile tucking in at the edges. Secretive.

That little giveaway made something like hope bloom in Gany's middle. "Has the other baker failed to deliver? Because we can set up now—"

"Not yet," Del said, tugging their jacket with hands that actually trembled. *Right. It's their wedding day.* "But soon."

"Will someone notify us then?"

"Trust me," they said, their palm on the swinging door once more, "you'll know. Now, if you'll excuse me, I need to get back to my guests"—their smile grew and now it was almost incandescent—"and my wife."

They vanished through the door.

Gany propped his hands on his hips. "What does that mean, *I'll know*? How am I supposed to know? Will there be a text? A bullhorn announcement? A freaking dove descending from on high?"

An enormous crash resounded from the ballroom, followed by shrieks and shouting and the pounding of many feet.

Finn quirked an eyebrow. "Call me Captain Obvious, but I think that's your cue."

Gany hurried over and pushed the swinging door open a crack, the others crowding behind him to peer over his shoulders.

The ballroom was in absolute chaos. At the far end, on the floor in front of a long, white-clothed table, was a huge, tumbled mess of dark chocolate and white buttercream, with the red of raspberry filling spackling it like blood spatter.

Two extremely handsome men crouched next to the mess, both in the white shirts, black waistcoats, and trousers of the catering staff. One of them—a stunning dark-skinned man, his completely bald head gleaming in the sunlight spilling in from the french doors—swiped a finger through the broken cake and popped it into his mouth.

The shouting at the door—which mostly seemed to be coming from a middle-aged woman in a lavender chiffon dress and a man of similar age in a tux—increased in volume. Somebody said something about the cake, and then Del, their arm around the waist of a willowy, high-cheekboned woman in a white body suit frosted with rainbow crystals from neck to ankles and a flounced overskirt edged with what looked like swansdown, smiled and met Gany's gaze across the ballroom.

"Oh, don't worry about that," they said, "I've got another one."

"Aaand *that's* our cue." Gany pointed to a nest of enormous plastic tubs on the shelf over a deep enamel sink. "Hector, Gage, Dakota, Finn. Please take those along with those bench scrapers and clean up the fallen cake." He turned to Peyton and Melina. "I'll carry the bottom layer. You two take the sixth and seventh. We'll assemble those and then come back for the top five tiers."

Without a single protest, everyone did exactly as Gany ordered. By the time he, Melina, and Peyton maneuvered the top layers into place—aided by Peyton's levitation spell, Nerida peeking bright eyes over the edge of their apron pocket—Finn and his friends had the floor in front of the table completely clean, the oak planks gleaming.

When Gany stood back to take it in for a moment, pride filling his chest, he heard a sharp intake of breath behind him. He turned to see the bride—Annemiek— gazing at the cake with shining eyes, Del at her side.

"It's beautiful," she murmured. "I'd never have thought of this but it's perfect. How did you know?" Then she laughed, a little wryly. "What am I saying? Of course you knew. You always know." She kissed Del's cheek. "That's what I get for marrying an oracle."

Gany blinked. *Oracle?* Finn's supe community wasn't limited to werewolves and witches?

Still… oracle. That explained *so much.*

Gany motioned to Peyton and Melina and they headed back to the kitchen, leaving the newlyweds with the photographer.

Peyton and Melina pushed through the door into the kitchen, but Gany waited, hands clasped under his chin, as the couple cut into the middle layer with the commemorative silver cake knife.

Finn joined him, kissing Gany's curls and wrapping an arm around his waist. "You did it, sweetheart."

"No, *we* did it. All of us. Peyton and Melina and I couldn't have managed without you and your friends—or Mr. Johnson and his crew." Gany slanted a glance at Finn. "I've already figured out that your supe community is bigger than I imagined. Del, apparently is an oracle."

Finn smiled down at him. "That's true."

"Any other secrets you can share with the class?"

"Well, Annemiek is a swan shifter."

Gany's jaw sagged. "Shut *up*. Seriously?"

Finn nodded, smirking. "You hit that one right on the head, without knowing anything about her, so kudos to your baker's intuition. Mr. Johnson is a beaver shifter, but he can't shift. He's married to a vampire."

Gany felt like his eyes were so wide now they might pop out of his head and roll across the floor. "Vampires?" he squeaked. "They're real?"

"Uh huh." Finn's gaze darted past Gany's shoulder and he gulped audibly. "And don't look now, but you're about to meet a demon."

The man hurrying across the ballroom toward them didn't look anything like what Gany imagined a demon would look. He was a little taller than Gany, his skin paler, his black curls shaggier, and he wore cute rectangular hipster glasses—in other words, just like a guy who'd pop into Nectar & Ambrosia any day of the week.

"Will he hurt us? Hurt you?" Gany asked, bracing himself just in case.

"Not physically. But I'm always waiting for the other shoe to drop when it comes to the consequences of my father's actions."

When the man reached them, though, he broke out into a sunny smile. "Finn! I couldn't believe it when I saw you. We've been trying to reach you for *ages*."

"Hey, Zeke. You have?" Finn edged a little closer to Gany, as if seeking comfort.

"Yes. We thought we could catch you when you came back to the hospital for your follow-up visit, but you haven't been in yet."

"Yeah. I've been, um, busy."

"Well, no matter. I've got you now." Even though Zeke's tone hadn't been cheerful rather than threatening, Gany felt Finn tense beside him. "There's a settlement."

"Shit." Finn's shoulders drooped and he scrubbed a hand over his face. "I was afraid of that. What do I owe?"

Zeke blinked, his eyes dark behind lenses that glinted with red highlights. "What? Oh. No, you don't understand. It's the council that owes *you*. A reward for exposing Patrick's schemes. You should have gotten it before you left the hospital the second time, but it got held up." He shrugged apologetically. "Apparently the exchange rate between Faerie gold and US dollars was in flux at the time."

Finn exchanged a glance with Gany before meeting Zeke's eyes. "How much?"

The amount Zeke named wasn't as much as the Fates had awarded Gany, but it was pretty damn close.

"Fuck," Finn muttered, leaning heavily against Gany.

"Anyway," Zeke said, "I've got to get back to my table. But stop by the Quest Investigations office on Monday and we'll get it sorted." He smiled at them both and then darted away.

"I can't believe it," Finn said. "I'm not broke anymore. I've got *options*."

Gany's heart tumbled and landed somewhere between his feet. "Of course. You'll probably want to get your own place now and—"

"What? No! It just means I won't be a parasite. I can *contribute*. I still want to be with you. See where we can go, what we can make of this thing between us. Besides..." He scrunched up his nose. "I kinda think the pups might have imprinted on me as their alpha, so there's that."

His heart now floating somewhere over his head, Gany laughed. "I got an email from TD yesterday. I forgot to tell you about it because I was hip deep in chocolate sponge at the time. He asked if I wanted to lease the house. It looks like he and Lonnie will be on location for longer than they thought and then they're moving to Toronto for a new TV series. His only worry was about the pups." Gany lifted on his toes and kissed Finn. "But it looks like that's taken care of."

"So you want it? This life? Me?"

"Honey, you couldn't be more perfect if Pygmalion had sculpted you just for me."

Finn bent down, but stopped before his mouth met Gany's, his gaze lifting to scan the ballroom. "We probably shouldn't steal the newlyweds' thunder by making out in the middle of their reception. Come on."

He laced his fingers with Gany's and tugged him through the door into the kitchen—where Frang and the rest of the crew were clustered around a prep table that held plastic tubs full of mangled cake and frosting. All of them looked up guiltily, buttercream and raspberry on their lips.

"What?" Frang said. "Nobody else wanted it."

"This is only from the top of the pile. We kept it separate from the stuff that touched the floor. Although," Hector popped a spoonful of cake and frosting into his mouth, "with weres," he said around the chocolate and buttercream, "there *is* no five-second rule."

Gany lifted a brow at Peyton and Melina. "What's your excuse?

Melina fluttered her eyelashes at him. "We had to scope out the competition, didn't we?"

Gany shook his head, laughing, just as the door to the main kitchen swung inward and Eros burst through it.

"Ganymede, look! I can't believe it. Your name is off the bonus quest list and I got all the points for it! I'm almost even with Hestia now and I didn't even *do* anything."

"You did something, Eros," Gany said with a smile. "You left us free to make our own choice. Just remember that lesson when you make it back up to Olympus."

Eros's dark eyes welled and he turned away.

"What's wrong?"

He sniffed, swiping under his nose with his sleeve. "You said *when*, not *if*. You really think I can make it?"

Finn draped his arm across Gany's shoulders. "Redemption is possible, as long as you learn from your mistakes." He glanced down at Gany, and the affection in his eyes... Gany's heart did a backflip. "It helps if you've got somebody at your back. Somebody who believes in you."

"Hmmm." Eros peered down at his phone again, then back up at Gany. "Where I can meet somebody like that?"

Gany shrugged. "Between Fates, oracles, werewolves, witches, demons, and who knows what else, there might be someone out there who's perfect for you too."

"If you— Hey! Is that cake?"

Eros shouldered in between Gage and Dakota, who offered him a spoon.

Finn kissed Gany's temple. "Does this mean the gods'll leave you alone?"

"It should." Gany glared at Eros's backside where he was bent over, shoveling cake into his mouth. "Because I'm not screwing around anymore. If any of them so much as poke their perfect noses into my bakery, I'm going straight to the Fates and lodging a complaint."

"Good. Because I don't want our lives to be overshadowed by the past—not yours, not mine, not my father's"—he jerked his chin at Eros—"and certainly not theirs." He smoothed Gany's curls off his forehead and kissed him softly. "Here's to restitution, redemption, and fresh starts."

"I'm game if you are." Gany returned the kiss, but then ducked his chin, heat rushing up his throat. "As long as, you know, you might need to wait a while before I'm ready for more *physically* than we're doing now."

"Sweetheart, take all the time you need, all the time in the world. As long as I'm with you, I'm happy to wait forever."

## a message from
### ej

Dear Reader,

Thank you so much for reading *At Odds with the Gods*, another paranormal rom-com with roots in my Mythmatched story world. I'm so happy you've taken this journey with me! I'd be immensely grateful if you'd take a moment to leave a review where you obtained the book and at any other site you use for reviews. Believe me, reviews make an *enormous* difference to the health and well-being of books (and not incidentally, to their associated authors!).

BTW, if you want to know why Del foresaw the need for another cake, you can find out all about what happens on the other side of the kitchen door in *Cursed is the Worst*.

My Mythmatched universe currently comprises—yikes! — more than twenty stories, but believe it or not, I've written in other worlds and other genres over twenty times as well! Pop on over to my website, https:// ejrussell.com, for all the deets on my books—my paranormal rom-coms and mysteries, my contemporary romances, and my one lone historical. If you're an audio fan, you can find the audio scoop there too. (The QR code on the next page will get you there with your smartphone camera or other code reader.)

Would you like exclusive content and ARC giveaways, not to mention gratuitous dance videos? Then I'd love for you to join me in E.J. Russell's Reality Optional, my Facebook fan group (https://facebook.com/groups/reality.optional). My newsletter is the place to get the latest dish on new releases, sales, and more. I promise I only send one out when I've got...well...news. You can subscribe here: https://ejrussell.com/newsletter.

All my best,
—E

## Also by ej

**Paranormal Romance**
***Mythmatched Universe***
*Fae Out of Water Trilogy*
Cutie and the Beast
The Druid Next Door
Bad Boy's Bard

*Supernatural Selection Trilogy*
Single White Incubus
Vampire With Benefits
Demon on the Down-Low

*Other Mythmatched Romances*
Howling on Hold
Possession in Session
Witch Under Wraps
Cursed is the Worst
The Skinny on Djinni
Assassin by Accident (part of Carnival of Mysteries)

*Quest Investigations Mysteries*
Five Dead Herrings
The Hound of the Burgervilles
The Lady Under the Lake
Death on Denial

At Odds with the Gods (A Mythmatched/Purgatory Playhouse crossover)

Mythmatchedlets (Mythmatched companion stories, free to newsletter subscribers in ebook form, collected in one paperback volume: *Second First Date, Rusty's Really Bad Day, First Flight, Getting the Band Together, Purgatory Postscript, A Very Quest Solstice*)

*Magic Emporium Series* (shared world)
Purgatory Playhouse

*Enchanted Occasions Series*
Best Beast
Nudging Fate
Devouring Flame

*Ghost Townies Series*
Ghostridden

*Legend Tripping Series*
Stumptown Spirits
Wolf's Clothing

*Art Medium Series*
The Artist's Touch
Tested in Fire
Art Medium: The Complete Collection (omnibus edition)

*Royal Powers Series* (shared world)
Duking It Out

Duke the Hall
King's Ex

**Science Fiction**
*Sun, Moon, and Stars Series*
Partnership
Principles

*Interdimensional Time Bureau*
Monster Till Midnight

**Historical Romance**
Silent Sin

**Contemporary Romance**
Camera Shy
Summer Kitchen
The Thomas Flair
Mystic Man
For a Good Time, Call... (A Bluewater Bay novel, with
Anne Tenino)

*Christmas Kisses* (holiday shorts)
The Probability of Mistletoe
An Everyday Hero
A Swants Soiree

*Geeklandia Series*
The Boyfriend Algorithm (M/F)
Clickbait

**Writing as Nelle Heran**

(traditional cozy mystery)

*Crafty Sleuth Series (with C.K. Eastland)*
Die Cut
Mixed Media
Found Objects (*coming soon*)

# About the
# *Author*

E.J. Russell (she/her), author of the award-winning Mythmatched paranormal romance series, writes LGBTQ+ romance and mystery in a rainbow of flavors. Count on high snark, low angst, and happy endings.

Reality? Eh, not so much.

She's married to Curmudgeonly Husband, a man who cares even less about sports than she does. Luckily, C.H. also loves to cook, or all three of their children (Lovely Daughter and Darling Sons A and B) would have survived on nothing but Cheerios, beef jerky, and Satsuma mandarins (the extent of E.J.'s culinary skill set).

E.J. also writes traditional cozy mystery as Nelle Heran. She lives in rural Oregon, enjoys visits from her wonderful adult children, and indulges in good books, red wine, and the occasional hyperbole.

*News & Social Media:*
Website: https://ejrussell.com
Newsletter: https://ejrussell.com/newsletter

# Acknowledgements

As committed an introvert as I am, I don't do this alone. Many, *many* thanks to lyric apted and the Crit Posse (L.C. Chase, Lee Blair, and Amy Aislin) for beta reading, whip-cracking, and hand-holding; to my long-suffering editor, Meg DesCamp (who's making a dartboard—or perhaps a drinking game—featuring all the words I reuse far too frequently); to my fabulous PA, NOLAKim, for boundless encouragement, humor, and patience.

To my family—Jim, Hana, Nick, Ross, and Billy—love and thanks for being there for me even when I'm clearly off wandering in another universe.

And, of course, to you, my readers. Your enthusiasm for my stories makes it possible for me to continue doing what I love.